James Gaffney

The ancient Irish church

Was it Catholic or Protestant?

James Gaffney

The ancient Irish church
Was it Catholic or Protestant?

ISBN/EAN: 9783741191916

Manufactured in Europe, USA, Canada, Australia, Japa

Cover: Foto ©Andreas Hilbeck / pixelio.de

Manufactured and distributed by brebook publishing software
(www.brebook.com)

James Gaffney

The ancient Irish church

THE ANCIENT IRISH CHURCH.

THE

ANCIENT IRISH CHURCH:

Was it Catholic or Protestant?

BY THE REV. JAMES GAFFNEY, C.C.

"The universal aptness of a religious system for all ages of
civilization, and for all sorts and conditions of men, well befit its
claim of divine origin. She is of all nations, and of all times, that
wonderful Church of Rome."—EOTHEN.

DUBLIN :

JAMES DUFFY, 15, WELLINGTON-QUAY,
AND
22, PATERNOSTER-ROW, LONDON.

1863.

DUBLIN:

Printed by J. M. O'Toole and Son,

7, GT. BRUNSWICK-STREET.

TO

THE VERY REV. LAURENCE DUNNE,

Archdeacon of the Diocese of Dublin,

THESE FEW PAGES, WHICH DIMLY SHADOW FORTH

THE FAITH OF OUR FATHERS,

Are Dedicated,

WITH SINCERE AND GRATEFUL ESTEEM.

PREFACE.

———

THE matter contained in the pages of this little volume has formed the substance of a lecture recently delivered before the Catholic Young Men's Society in Dublin. I have aimed at nothing more than bringing together witnesses of learning and impartiality to testify to historical facts. Such attempts have been latterly made to obscure and pervert the truth, that it may not be amiss to direct attention to authentic documents, which set forth, plainly and simply, the dogmas of our Ancient Church. The authorities referred to are Irish manuscripts, dating back to the earliest period of our Christian history, and the writings of

our distinguished antiquaries—mostly Protestant—men of undoubted learning and unques-
tioned honor. Their testimony will assuredly
outweigh with an enlightened public the con-
fident declamations of Skinner's-alley.

Much more could be readily made of the
subject I have endeavoured to epitomise. There
is, however, so great an indisposition to study
any period of Irish history, that one is quite
afraid to enter too largely upon a theme, which
may not prove as interesting to the general
public, as it is to the clerical student.

Those who desire to examine fully the questions here barely touched upon, can easily find
abundant stores of information in Lanigan's
Ecclesiastical History, in the works issued by
the Irish Archæological Society, and, above all,
in O'Curry's MS. Materials of Irish History.
Had the Catholic University no other claims
upon our support than the publication of
O'Curry's work, it has done enough to endear

it to every Irish Catholic. That volume contains a mine of richest lore, hitherto unworked ; and from every page, the precious metal sparkles, encouraging the earnest seeker after truth to pursue labours which will bring him most valuable results. To those who may not have money to spend upon expensive books, yet would willingly desire to soothe the day's hard labour by an hour's occasional reading about old Catholic Ireland, I would venture to recommend the penny Lives of the Irish Saints, published by Mr. Duffy. They are full of interesting facts, arranged by no unskilful hand, and have merits far beyond the unpretending form in which they are presented to the public.

J. G.

Malahide,
FEAST OF ST. GALL, 1863.

CONTENTS.

THE RELIGION

OF

THE ANCIENT IRISH CHURCH.

CHAPTER I.

A LOVE of Fatherland is implanted in the human breast by God, and being a portion of our nature, is to be found in every clime, and under every variety of circumstance. In a prosperous nation, like England, it is the strongest bulwark of the people's liberties. By creating and fostering self-respect, it at once resists domestic tyranny, and repels foreign invasion. In countries whose Nationality has been trampled down by the heel of the conqueror,—such as in Poland, and in other lands with which we, Irishmen, may be more familiar,—it refuses to blot out the characteristics of its own national existence, and seeks, amidst its trials and tears, to preserve the national language, traditions, and history. We, the inhabitants of this Green Isle, love the country of our birth; yet it is most

B

strange how our love of Fatherland, or patriotism, as it is called, does so little prompt us to study the records of that country. At school we are taught the histories of Rome, Greece, and England, but not one word about Ireland. In the studies we pursue during our maturer years, how small a share of our time is spent in making familiar, as household words, the events which make up the life of our country! The general apathy which prevails with regard to the subject of Irish history, is traceable to two causes. In the first place, as to the educated classes, we have no Catholic literature fit for their perusal ; we have had no Catholic University till within a few years past; hence, we have not books written with ability and learning, which would bring before us, in its true light, the real history of this old Catholic land. In the second place, as to the humbler classes, a system of National Education has been concocted for them, which carefully excludes from its teaching any allusion calculated to instruct them, as Irishmen, in a love of Fatherland, or to move them, as Catholics, to emulate, in the preservation of their faith, the memorable achievements of early Christian Ireland, or the unbending firmness under persecution by which our ancestors preserved, for three hundred years, our creed pure and un-

sullied, and handed it to us, their children, to trans-
mit, as the dearest and best inheritance to those who
shall come after us. Some persons allege, as an excuse
for their neglect of the study of their country's annals,
that we have no history to study—that our history is
still to to be acted. That this is, in a great measure,
true of our nation for some centuries past—namely,
since the English invasion—is, alas! undeniable; yet
was there a time when Ireland was the most illustrious country in Europe; and during four hundred
years she continued the school of the West, and the
centre from which was diffused, through the continent
of Europe, civilization, learning, and religion. Of
this period, Dr. Johnson says: "Leland begins his
history too late;* the ages which deserve inquiry are
those times, *for such there were*, when Ireland was the
school of the West—the quiet habitation of sanctity
and literature."†

It is, then, incumbent upon us, as Irishmen, to
know the history of those times, to study it deeply,
to pore over the pages which recount these glories
of the Emerald Isle, and, moreover, to study them
before we attend to the history of any other nation,—

---

* Leland's History commences with the time of Henry II., in
the twelfth century.

† Boswell's Life.

in the words of Whiteside, "Ireland first, everything else afterwards,"—the best thing that versatile gentleman ever uttered.

We are all aware that Ireland was anciently called the "Island of Saints," and that this remarkable title was given her, not through a spirit of egotism by her own children, but by all the countries of Europe to which her sons bore the torches of learning and religion. Upon another occasion we may inquire into the claims of Ireland as a literary nation, passing in review her colleges, the lives of the distinguished men produced in them, and the services rendered by Irish professors to the cause of learning. On the present occasion, we shall confine ourselves to investigating the nature of that religion taught and practised in the early Irish Church—a religion which produced such multitudes of holy men and women, as to win from admiring and grateful Europe the proud title of "Island of Saints."

There is a noisy class of Protestants in Ireland, and especially in the city of Dublin, who proclaim, from pulpit and platform, in the press and in debates, that the religion which threw such a halo of glory round Ireland, for four centuries after the introduction of Christianity, was not the Catholic

religion at all, but on the contrary, that it was the
pure Protestantism taught in Townsend-street by
Rev. Mr. Eade, or in Fishamble-street by the re-
doubtable champion Rev. C. F. M'Carthy. The
latest exponent of those views is the Right Hon.
James Whiteside, who, although scarcely recovered
from his enlightened exertions to deprive poor Catholic prisoners in England of the ministrations of
their clergy, yet unsparingly taxes his energies to
convince the House of Commons that the Catholic
religion is an innovation in Ireland, whilst the Established Church, whose enormous revenues he wishes
to remain untouched, is the real ancient church of
Ireland. His words, as reported in the London
Times, of May 20th, are as follows:—"If I were
asked to say why I maintain that branch of the
church which exists in Ireland, my answer would
be, plainly and directly, that I maintain it because I
believe it upholds the ancient, pure, Catholic faith
which was professed in Ireland centuries before the
English set foot in that country. The ablest scholars, the best divines, the soundest antiquaries, are
agreed upon that point; and no man has proved it
more logically, or more conclusively, than Canon
Wordsworth, in the series of discourses which he
delivered in Westminster Abbey, for the purpose of

establishing our claim to be the true descendants of the ancient Catholic Church in Ireland. That man is profoundly ignorant who attacks the ancient church in Ireland. The question between us and the Roman Catholics is, which of us most nearly conforms to that church? Few will venture to deny that the argument of the divine who compared the ancient creed with that which we repeat every Sabbath-day—who showed that the Nicene Creed agrees, in substance, with that established by St. Patrick—was conclusive; and, therefore, I maintain that the church in Ireland preserves the old, ancient, true, Catholic faith " (cheers).

Here we at once join issue with Mr. Whiteside. He carries into the debate all the partiality of the advocate. He states, in the first place, that the Protestant Church is the ancient Church of Ireland: that we deny, and shall undertake to disprove. In the next place, he alleges that " the ablest scholars, the best divines, and the soundest antiquaries, *are agreed* upon that point." The untruth of this assertion is only equalled by its audacity. Did O'Donovan, the greatest Irish antiquarian of the age, agree to it? No. Did O'Curry, only second to O'Donovan, whose place as an historian of ancient Ireland no one living can fill,—did he agree to it? Here is his answer, in reference to the "Canon of St. Patrick," of which hereafter. "This most important canon affords a proof so unanswerable, as to dispose for ever of the modern imposition so pertinaciously practised upon a large section of our countrymen, as well as upon foreigners speaking the English language—namely, that the primitive Church of Erin did not acknowledge or submit to the Pope's supremacy, or appeal to it in cases of ecclesiastical difficulty. Nor is this canon, I may add, by any means the only piece of important evidence furnished by our ancient books on this great point of Catholic doctrine."* And yet, in the face of such writings, Mr. Whiteside has the coolness to assert that the soundest antiquarians, and the ablest scholars, *are agreed* upon this point—that the Protestant Church is the ancient Church of Ireland.

As a contrast to such amusing simplicity, we turn, with pleasure, to acknowledge how much Ireland is indebted, for the knowledge of her early Christian history, to the enlightened labours of Dr. Todd, of Trinity College; Dr. Reeves, Rector of Lusk; of Dr. Graves, Dean of the Chapel Royal; and of Dr. Petrie, the illustrious author of the most able work

* MS. Materials of Irish History, p. 373.

which has been published on the Round Towers
of Ireland. To the writings of these men we shall
constantly appeal, as they are witnesses above all
suspicion of partiality to the Catholic Church, but
men whose love of historic truth will not allow itself
to be warped or blinded by narrow prejudice, whilst
their learning has familiarised them with the genuine
facts of Irish history.

The question then before us is as to a mere matter
of fact. What religion did St. Patrick teach? What
did his followers practise? What dogmas were believed in that Church, which was the fruitful mother
of countless hosts of the learned and religious sons
of Erin, from the time of Ireland's Apostle, St.
Patrick, till the invasions of Danes, at the close of
the eighth, or of the English, at the close of the
twelfth century?

The principal doctrines that essentially separate
the Catholic Church from the Protestant Church
are:—

1. The real presence of Christ in the most holy
Eucharist, and the sacrifice of the Body and Blood
of Christ in the Mass.

2. The power of absolving from sin, exercised in
the Sacrament of Penance, and consequently the
practice of confession.

3. Prayers for the dead, and the doctrine of Purgatory.

4. Constant use of the sign of the cross, and miracles.

5. Veneration for the saints, and the practice of asking their prayers—including a special reverence for the Mother of God.

6. The necessity for mortification and penance, as shown forth in the laws of the Church, enjoining fasts during Lent, and at other seasons.

7. The supremacy of the Pope, as successor of St. Peter.

8. As a *matter of discipline*, the celibacy of the clergy; the practice of reciting the Divine Office, and the strict observance of Holidays, as well as Sundays.

9. Absolute belief in and profound reverence for the sacred Scriptures.

If it shall be proved that such were the doctrines of the Early Irish Church, and such its discipline, it must be admitted that the claims of latter-day Protestants to that Early Church are not as conclusive as Mr. Whiteside would have us believe.

Before we proceed to discuss each of these points in detail, let us take a *coup d'œil* of the Church founded by St. Patrick. The general outlines are so repugnant to every idea of Protestantism, that the most superficial glance is sufficient to convince an impartial inquirer of the futility of claiming that Early Church to have had any resemblance to the Established Church or to any form of Protestantism.

St. Patrick began his mission in Ireland in A.D. 432, having been sent to preach the faith here by Pope Celestine, as his predecessor, St. Palladius, had also been. He spent thirty-three years in the conversion of the Irish, and was eminently successful in every province, and every part of Ireland which he visited. Towards the close of his mission, he settled at Armagh; built a church there, which he made the head church of Ireland, and beside that primatial church, he erected a monastery.

St. Patrick had spent many years of his life preparing for the sacred ministry, in a monastery, under his near relative, St. Martin, Bishop of Tours. He had afterwards repaired to another establishment of the same character in the island of Lerins, in the Tuscan Sea. Treasuring in his mind a lively remembrance of the years which he passed in pursuit of virtue within these hallowed enclosures, he had no sooner ceased from his travels throughout Ireland, and settled at Armagh, than he surrounds himself with a monastery for the education of his priests, and

the asylum of his old age.* The example set by
St. Patrick was speedily followed by his successors,
and immediately monasteries and nunneries arose in
every part of the land. St. Bridget, who was born
several years before St. Patrick's death, became a
nun; she received the veil at the hands of the Bishop
of Westmeath, the Right Rev. P. Maccaille,† a name.
not unknown in Irish history. She, like St. Patrick,
travelled through all the provinces of Ireland, founding nunneries on every side, and eventually settled
down at Kildare, where, after a long life of 75 years,
she closed her eyes in peace in the midst of her nuns.
"Innumerable convents of women," writes Montalembert,‡ "trace their origin to the Abbess of Kildare; wherever the Irish monks have penetrated,
from Cologne to Seville, churches have been raised
in her honour, and wherever, in our own time, British
emigration spreads, the name of Bridget points out
the woman of Irish race. Deprived by persecution
and poverty of the means of erecting monuments of
stone, they testify their unshaken devotion to that
dear memory, by giving her name to their daughters

* Accepit ergo ab eo (Daire) Stus. Patricius prœdium optatum
et placitum sibi, et ædificavit in eo *monasteria* religiosorum
virorum.—Probus, l. 3, c. 7; Lanigan, vol. i. p. 314.
† Lanigan, vol. i. p. 385.
‡ Monks of the West, vol. ii. p. 394.

—a noble and touching homage, made by a race always unfortunate and always faithful to a saint, who was like itself a slave,* and like itself a Catholic. There are glories more noisy and splendid, but are there many which do more honour to human nature?" Whilst she was so successfully engaged in establish-.ing and governing her various communities of holy virgins, earnest men, anxious about heavenly things, are crowding into monasteries, and forming those towns, many of which, like Derry, now despise the memory and ridicule the superstition of their founders. Immense communities of monks are gathered at Bangor, under St. Comgall; at Moville, under St. Finian; at Clonard, under another St. Finian; at Clonfert, under St. Brendan; and at Clonmacnoise, under St. Kieran. "These sixth-century monasteries," says Dr. Reeves,† " were as rapid in their growth as they were numerous in their creation. St. Finian's, of Clonard; St. Comgall's, of Bangor; and St. Brendan's, of Clonfert; each numbered 3,000 inmates."

It is admitted on all hands by Irish historians, as will be proved in due course, that all these monks and nuns were bound by vows of celibacy, and that

---

* This is incorrect ; she was of noble descent at both sides. See Lanigan, vol. i. p. 378.

† Reeves' Notes to Adamnan's Life of St. Columbkille, p. 336.

they fasted most severely. What then is there in this faithful picture of the Early Church of Ireland that bears the shadow of resemblance to the Established Church, or to any form of Protestantism? Have they monks? do they not stigmatise them? Have they nuns? do they not ridicule the silliness of those ladies, who give up the world to spend their days in solitude with God? Is there, on the other hand, any discordance between these institutions of early Ireland and the Catholic Church of to-day? Not the least. We have our monasteries and our convents, as well as the Irish of the time of St. Patrick, St. Bridget, and St. Columbkille.

We now proceed to consider in detail each of those points, which mark the clear boundaries between Catholicity and Protestantism.

1. The most holy Eucharist and the Mass:—What was the teaching of the Early Irish Church on the Real Presence, and the Sacrifice of the Mass?

The most valuable Life of St. Patrick which is extant is that by Probus. In it we read* that St. Patrick, in his tour through Connaught, converted two daughters of King Leogaire, Ethnea and Fethlimia. In answer to their desire of seeing Christ face

* Probus, l. ii. c. 15; quoted by Lanigan, Eccl. Hist., vol. i. p. 241-243.

to face, he told them that Eucharistic communion
was one of the necessary requisites with regard to
that object; upon which they said, "Give us the
Sacrifice of the Body and Blood of Christ, that we
may be freed from the corruption of the flesh, and
see our spouse, who is in heaven." And St. Patrick
then celebrating Mass, they received the holy Eucharist. One of these ladies afterwards applied to St.
Patrick, and became a nun.

In the festology of Aengus (a manuscript of the
eighth century), at the 13th of April, Bishop Tassach,
one of St. Patrick's favourite companions, is thus
commemorated:—" The kingly Bishop Tassach, who
administered on his arrival, *the Body of Christ,
the truly powerful King, and the Communion to St.
Patrick.*"*

Hence, it appears that Bishop Tassach attended St.
Patrick when dying, and administered to him, as
viaticum,

"The Body of Christ, the truly powerful King."

A statement to the same effect is also given in the
tripartite life of St. Patrick.†

---

* O'Curry's MS. Materials of Irish Hist., p. 368. Lanigan,
vol. i. p. 346.

† Apud Colgan Trias Thaumat. p. 168. See O'Donovan's Annals F. M., vol. i. p. 157.

We learn from the annotations of Tirechan, written in the seventh century, and contained in the Book of Armagh, that the anniversary of St. Patrick's death was celebrated—1st. By reciting his hymn; 2ndly. By offering the *proper Mass* on that day—" Offertorium ejus proprium in eodem die immolari," which Dr. Todd thus explains—" The second mark of respect paid to St. Patrick was a special offertorium to his honor on the day of his festival." The meaning seems to be, that a special commemoration of him should be made in the " Preface of the Mass," beginning " vere dignum et justum est," which, in the Gothic and ancient Gallican Missals, was termed " Immolatio Missæ," and in which the proper prefaces, commemorative of festivals and saints' days, are introduced."* The commemoration of St. Patrick, thus introduced, occurred in the prayer which immediately follows the proper prefaces, and commences with the words " Communicantes," &c.

St. Patrick died in 465.† Benignus was immediately elected his successor, and died in 468. Finding his end approaching, he sent for St. Jarlath, and received from him the *Lord's Body.* St.

---

* Dr. Todd's Notes to the Liber Hymnorum, p. 51.

† Some maintain that he died much later. See Annals of Four Masters, vol. i. p. 157 ; also Haverty's Hist. of Ireland, p. 71.

Benignus died on 9th November, and was buried at
Armagh. " Cum vir Dei (Benignus) viderit tem-
pus suæ resolutionis instare, curat accersiri sanctam
Hierlatium .... et ex ejus manu arrham et pignus
æterne beatitudinis *Corpus Domini* devotissime sumit,
et se ad vitæ terminum et Patriæ parat introitum."[*]

" When the man of God (Benignus) saw that the
time of his dissolution was near at hand, he sent for
St. Jarlath ... and received most devoutly from his
hand the earnest and pledge of eternal happiness—
namely, the Body of Christ; and thus prepared himself for death and for his entrance into his country."

The same doctrine of the Early Irish Church on
the Blessed Eucharist, is set forth as the belief of
the illustrious St. Bridget. A valuable life of this
saint, by Cogitosus, has come down to us. The
work is assigned by "the soundest antiquaries"—
namely, Petrie, O'Donovan, and Lanigan, to the early
part of the ninth century.[†] In this genuine history,
we have a description of the church founded at
Kildare, by St. Bridget, and in which she and her
nuns were accustomed to assemble for Mass and
other devotions. As the saint was, at least, twelve

---

[*] Vita St. Benigni, c. 18 ; quoted by Lanigan, vol. i. p. 375.
[†] Round Towers, p. 197 ; Annals of Four Masters, vol. i. p.
172 ; Lanigan, vol. i. p. 379.

years of age at the death of St. Patrick, and lived to
establish convents throughout the entire of Ireland,
'tis manifest her faith was that of Christian Ireland
in the days of our apostle. Now listen to those
words, taken from her life, by Cogitosus, and quoted
by Dr. Petrie in his work on the Round Towers of
Ireland; they refer to her church*—" And through
the one door, placed on the right side (of the church
of Kildare), the chief prelate entered the sanctuary,
accompanied by his regular school, and those who
are deputed to the sacred ministry of offering *sacred*
and *dominical sacrifices*. Through the other door,
.... none enter but the abbess, with her virgins
and widows, among the faithful, when going to par·
ticipate in the banquet of the *Body* and *Blood of
Jesus Christ*."

There can be no question of the genuineness of
this extract. Let us ask, then, is this description of
the church attached to the convent of Kildare,
such as would suit any house of Protestant worship?
Passing back in spirit through 1300 years, we behold
the assembly of the faithful gathered round God's
altar for solemn worship; on one side the prelate,
accompanied by those who are deputed to the sacred
ministry of offering sacred and dominical sacrifices,

* Round Towers, p. 197·8; Trans. R.I.A.

c

on the other side enters the procession of holy virgins arrayed in white,* and following the great foundress of their Order, to participate in "the banquet of the Body and Blood of Jesus Christ." And yet, in the face of such historical portraiture, we are assured that "the ablest scholars, the best divines, and the soundest antiquaries are agreed" in making out that these holy recluses were all staunch Protestants like Mr. Whiteside.

St. Bridget having governed her convents for several years, at last prepares to pay the universal debt of Nature; and, in order to strengthen herself for the dread passage from death to eternity, she, like St. Patrick and St. Benignus, receives, a short time before her death, the Communion of the Body and Blood of our Lord from the hand of St. Nennidh,† and expires in the 75th year of her age, A.D. 525.

In a little work, entitled the "Saintly Triad," and comprising the lives of St. Patrick, St. Bridget, and St. Columbkille, by a Protestant Clergyman, the death of St. Bridget is recorded in these words: "She departed this life in Kildare, at the age of seventy, or thereabouts, having previously received the Holy Communion 'of the Body and Blood of our Lord

---

* Cogitosus, cap. 3, quoted by Lanigan, vol. i. p. 385.
† 4th Life, b. 2, c. 63, quoted by Lanigan, vol. i. p. 456.

Jesus Christ, the Son of the living God,' as her biographer informs us."[*]

ST. COLUMBKILLE.

Four years before the death of St. Brigid, one of the most distinguished saints which this country ever produced was born at Gartan, near Letterkenny, in the County of Donegal. St. Columba, or Columb-kille, is the name of the third of Ireland's patron saints. The life of this celebrated man was written by Adamnan, a monk of Columbkille's own Order, and his successor in the abbacy of Iona. The work was compiled about eighty-three years after the saint's death.[†] It is admitted by all writers on Irish history to be a faithful record of Columbkille and his times. It has been recently published for the Archæological Society, and illustrated with most learned notes by the Rev. Dr. Reeves, Rector of Lusk.

This life, then, being a trustworthy witness of the teachings of the Early Irish Church, is a most conclusive authority as to the doctrines of that Church in the ages immediately succeeding that of St. Patrick. Now, to resume—What was believed rela-

---

[*] See 4th Life, book 2nd, c. 63 ; p. 178 of the "Triad."
[†] Rev. J. King's Church Hist. vol. i. p. 88.

tive to the Blessed Eucharist and the Sacrifice of the
Mass in the time of St. Columbkille? Dr. Reeves *
says, in one of his copious notes under the head of
" Divine Worship ": " The Dies Solemnes were the
Sundays and Holydays (Sanctorum Natales) which
were solemnized in the same manner, by rest from
labour, the celebration of the Eucharist, and the use
of better food. . . . . The stated services were *Mass*,
Matins, Prime, Tierce, Sext and probably None.†
In the ' Sacra Eucharistiæ Ministeria ' (210), also
called ' Sacra Mysteria' (211-221), 'Sacræ Oblationis
Mysteria' (77), wine (104) and water, which was
drawn by the deacon, and bread (85) were provided;
the priest (77) standing before the altar (222) proceeded to consecrate,—Sacræ Eucharistiæ Consecrare
Mysteria (221), Sacram oblationem Consecrare (222)
Sacræ Eucharistiæ Mysteria Conficere (77), Christi
Corpus Conficere (85). . . . . The brethren then
approached the altar, and partook of the Eucharist."‡
In these words of Dr. Reeves, commenting on the
life of St. Columbkille, we learn how the Irish
monks, at home in Derry, in Clonard, and Durrow,

---

* Adamnan's Life of St. Columba, p. 346.

† In another place, p. 77-182, he says, " the chief service-books
were the *Missals* and *Office*-books."

‡ The figures refer to the pages in Adamnan, where the words
quoted are found.

as well as in Iona, passed their Sundays: "they recited the Divine Office, and celebrated Mass, at which they consecrated the sacred mysteries of the Eucharist, and 'made the Body of Christ,' whilst the lay monks, at the end of the Mass, received the Blessed Eucharist." We should like to know what Mr. Whiteside has to say to this admission of one of " the soundest antiquaries " of his own church.

Again: " we read"* says Dr. Reeves, " in the Life of St. Brendan of Clonfert, that he was ordered to celebrate Mass, by St. Gildas, the abbot of the monastery. The 'custos templi,' (*i. e.*, monk in charge of the church—the sacristan) said to him 'præcepit tibi sanctus senex noster, ut *offeras Corpus Christi*. Ecce Altare, hunc librum Græcis litteris scriptum, et canta in ea sicut abbas noster.—Our holy Superior commands you to offer the Body of Christ. Here is the altar, and the missal written in Greek characters —chant in it as our abbot does.'"

Again, in Adamnan's Life of St. Columbkille, we are told that a Munster bishop named Cronan, was ordered by the saint to celebrate Mass " Nam alia Die Dominica a Sancto jussus *Christi Corpus ex more conficere.*" " Upon Sunday he was ordered by St. Columba to make the Body of Christ according to

* Vitæ Columbæ, notes, p. 354.

the usual practice." Now we are to bear in mind that St. Columbkille was brought up in a monastery in the Co. Down (Moville); that he afterwards studied in the monastery of Clonard, and there associated with those men who are called the Fathers of the Early Church;[*] that he founded several monasteries before he went to Iona, and that the teaching and practices of the monks at Iona were identically the same as those of the Irish monasteries, from which these monks went forth under Columbkille's guidance. Hence what is said of his monks holds true of the monasteries which were founded by his companions and fellow-students, and were spread in his time through the length and breadth of Ireland.

ANTIPHONARY OF BANGOR.

One of the most celebrated of the Irish monasteries was that of Bangor, near Belfast. When King Alfred the Great founded or restored the University of Oxford, he is stated to have sent to Bangor for professors, so great was the reputation for learning then enjoyed by the monks of this establishment. There is extant a manuscript of the eighth century, entitled the " Antiphonary of Ban-

---

[*] The two Brendans of Clonfert and Birr, the Kierans, &c. &c.

gor "; it was written in this famous monastery, brought thence to Bobbio in the north of Italy, and found by Cardinal Borromeo in the library of the Irish establishment formed there by another distinguished countryman of ours, St. Columbanus.* It is now preserved in the Ambrosian library at Milan. In this Antiphonary is contained a Hymn entitled " Hymnus quando communicarent sacerdotes." It is printed in the Liber Hymnorum, edited by Todd, and is as follows :

THE COMMUNION HYMN.

1.

Sancti venite,

Christi Corpus sumite,

Sanctum bibentes

Quo redempti sanguinem.

1.

† Draw nigh, ye holy ones, draw nigh,

And take the body of the Lord,

And drink the Sacred Blood outpoured,

By which redeemed ye shall not die.

2.

Salvati Christi

Corpore et sanguine,

A quo refecti,

Laudes dicamus Deo.

2.

Oh! saved from justice and the rod,

By this divinest Flesh and Blood,

By these made strong in grateful mood,

Give thanks and praises unto God.

---

* Lanigan's Preface, viii. ; also vol. i. p. 59.

† I am indebted for this beautiful translation to Mr. Denis Florence M'Carthy.

3.

Hoc sacramento

Corporis et sanguinis,

Omnes exuti

Ab inferni faucibus.

3.

By this (oh! blessed news to
tell !)
This sacrament of Flesh and
Blood
Have all been rescued from the
flood—
The flood of death—the pains of
hell.

4.

Dator salutis

Christus filius Dei,

Mundum salvavit

Per crucem et sanguinem.

4.

The Giver of Salvation, He
The Christ, the Son of God
above,
Restored unto his Father's
love
The world, by Blood and by
the Tree.

5.

Pro universis

Immolatus Dominus,

Ipse sacerdos

Existit et hostia.

5.

For all of every clime and coast,
The Lord is offered up to
Heaven ;
For all the Sacrifice is given,
Himself at once the priest and
host.

6.

Lege præceptum

Immolari hostias,

Qua adumbrantur

Divina mysteria,

6.

Read well the story through and
through,
Of victims bleeding at the
shrine,
Types of a mystery more divine,
And shadows of a truth more
true.

7.

Lucis indultor,

Et salvator omnium,

Præclaram sanctis

Largitus est gratiam.

7.

The liberal Giver of all light,

The Saviour of the human race,
A special glory and a grace

Doth give his Saints who fear his might.

8.

Accedant omnes,

Pura mente creduli,

Sumant æternam

Salutis custodiam.

8.

Approach ye all with fond and pure
Believing hearts, and, for His sake,
The gage of your salvation, take
Your soul's physician and its cure.

9.

Sanctorum custos,

Rector quoque Dominus,

Vitæ perennis

Largitor credentibus.

9.

The Guardian of the Saints, the Lord,
By whom ye move, and breathe, and live,
Eternal life doth largely give

To those believing in his word.

10.

Celestem panem

Dat esurientibus,

De fonte vivo

Prebet sitientibus.

10.

The bread of heaven he doth bestow
On hungry souls about to sink;

The thirsty he permits to drink

From out a living fountain's flow.

11.	11.
Alpha et Omega,	The Source and Stream, the First and Last,
Ipse Christus Dominus	Even Christ the Lord who died for men,
Venit, venturus	Now comes—but he will come again,
Judicare homines.	To judge the world, when time hath passed.

The Book of Armagh, which was written in 807, contains a notice of this hymn—on which Dr. Todd remarks:*—"This curious notice is valuable from its antiquity, and proves beyond all reasonable doubt that the hymn was known, and its recitation enjoined as a pious practice, as early as the close of the eight century in Ireland."

This beautiful exposition of Catholic faith and devotion, recited in the Early Irish Church, shows us convincingly how perfect is the accordance of the Catholic faith of to-day in Ireland with what it was in the first ages of Christianity in this country.

ANCIENT TREATISE ON THE MASS.

The late Professor O'Curry, in his invaluable lectures, delivered at the Catholic University,† describes an Ancient Treatise upon or Explication of the Symbolical Ceremonies of the Mass in Latin and

* Liber Hymnorum, Notes, p. 50.
† MS. Material of Irish History, p. 376.

Gaedlic, and a powerful exposition of the doctrine of
the Eucharistic Sacrifice. The following extract, he
writes, is literally translated from the tract I have
referred to:—

"Another division of that pledge, which has been
left to the Church to comfort her, is the Body of Christ
and His Blood, which are offered upon the altars of the
Christians. The Body, even, which was born of Mary,
Immaculate Virgin, without destruction of her vir-
ginity, without opening of the womb, without presence
of man; and which was crucified by the unbelieving
Jews, out of spite and envy, and which arose after
three days from death, and sits upon the right hand
of God the Father in heaven, in glory and in dignity
before the angels of heaven;—it is that Body, the
same as it is in this great glory, which the righteous
consume off God's Table, that is, the holy altar.
For this Body is the rich viaticum of the faithful,
who journey through the paths of pilgrimage and
penitence of this world to the heavenly fatherland.
This is the seed of the Resurrection in the Life Eternal to the righteous. It is, however, the origin and
cause of falling to the impenitent, who believe not,
and to the sensual, who distinguish it not, though
they believe. Woe then to the Christian who distinguishes not this Holy Body of the Lord by pure

morals, by charity, and by mercy. For it is in this
Body that will be found the example of the charity
which excels all charity, viz., to sacrifice Himself,
without guilt, in satisfaction for the guilt of the
whole race of Adam."

" This, then, is the perfection of the Catholic Faith,
as it is taught in the Holy Scriptures."

The original is contained in the Leabhar Breac,
which is deposited in the Royal Irish Academy.

On this extract O'Curry remarks:—"The passage
which I have translated for you is short, but even
were it a little longer, I think you would excuse
me when you find in it a complete and undeniable
proof of what it is the fashion of Protestant writers
to deny without any reason, namely, that the belief
of our Gaedlic ancestors respecting the Real Presence,
and all the meaning of the Holy Sacrifice of the
Mass, was in the early ages of the Church in Erinn,*
precisely the same belief now held by ourselves, precisely the same belief inculcated then as now, by the
Catholic Church throughout the world." We com-
mend this passage to Mr. Whiteside's notice, especially
when he next undertakes to prove that the Early

---

* O'Curry also observes that the late Rev. Dr. Kelly considered
it to be the Mass brought into Ireland by St. Patrick, and that the
Gaedlic part of the tract is of the purest and most ancient Christian
character.—MS., p. 377.

Irish Church was the same as the present Established Church in Ireland, because they both received the Nicene Creed. This profound and original argument would equally show that the Catholic Church of to-day, or, as he would call it, the Roman Catholic Church and the Protestant Established Church were precisely identical, because the Nicene Creed is recited every Sunday at Mass, and forms also a portion of Protestant worship!

Ussher published a treatise entitled "The Religion of the Ancient Irish." In it he undertook the desperate task of proving that the religion of Ireland in the days of St. Patrick was the same as that of the Protestant Church. It is really amusing to observe how he endeavours to get over the difficulties about the Blessed Eucharist. " We may observe," he writes, " in the first place, that the public liturgy or service of the Church was of old named the Mass; even then also when prayers were only said, without the celebration of the Holy Communion. 'The last Mass that St. Columba was ever present at,' says Adamnan, ' was the Vesper Mass of the Lord's Day.' But the name of the Mass was in those days more especially applied to the administration of the Lord's Supper, and, therefore, in the same Adamnan we see that ' the Sacred Mystery of the Eucharist' and ' the

solemnities of the Mass' are taken for the same thing.
So, likewise, in the relation of the passages that con-
cern the obsequies of Columbanus, performed by
Gallus and Magnoaldus, we find 'the saying of Mass'
was the same with ' the celebration of the Divine
Mysteries and the oblation of the healthful sacrifice;' for by that term was the administration of the
Sacrament of the Lord's Supper at that time usually
designated."*

Who ever heard of a Protestant clergyman " saying Mass" as the Early Irish priests and monks did,
according to Ussher? Were not our churches and
chapels lately—are they not sometimes even now—
called " Mass-houses" as a term of derision? But
Dr. Reeves, in a passage already quoted, tells us what
the Mass was in ancient Ireland; namely, that " on
Sundays and holidays Mass was said; that the priest,
having provided bread, wine, and water, stood before
the altar, and there proceeded to consecrate the sacred
mysteries, and to make the Body of Christ—Conficere Corpus Christi."

A remarkable " Catalogue of the Early Irish Saints"
was published by Ussher from ancient manuscripts,
in his " Antiquities of the British Churches."† It is

---

* Religion of Ancient Irish.
† Ussher's Works, vol. vi. c. xvii. p. 477.

considered by all antiquaries as a very valuable document, which throws great light on our ancient ecclesiastical history. It is given in full in King's Church History of Ireland.[*] "This document," says Dr. Lanigan,[†] "bears every mark of high antiquity, and was most probably drawn up some time before the disputes about the Paschal cycle and the tonsure had totally subsided, which was not until about the year 716." The document is, therefore, one of the seventh century, or beginning of the eight, as Rev. Mr. King admits. Archbishop Ussher does not say to what age its composition is to be attributed; but it was probably written at a very early period—the beginning, perhaps, of the eighth century, as the author brings down his list no farther than to the year 664."[‡] We give the account of this Catalogue which occurs in Mr. King's History. "According to this Catalogue, then, the Irish Saints are divided into three classes, of which the first order was most holy, the second order, very holy; the third, holy. The first was like the blazing sun, the second like the moon, the third like the stars.

" The first order of Catholic Saints was in the time

---

[*] Church History of Ireland, by Rev. R. King, vol. i. p. 59.
[†] Lanigan, Eccl. Hist. vol. ii. p. 14.
[‡] King's Hist. vol. i. p. 62.

of Patrick.   And then all the bishops, to the number
of 350, who were also founders of churches, were
eminent and holy, and full of the Holy Spirit. They
had one head, Christ; and one leader, Patrick—*one
Mass, one mode of celebration*, one tonsure from ear to
ear."

This order of Saints extended over four reigns, that
is, from St. Patrick in 432 to 534, or upwards of 100
years.

"The second order of Catholic presbyters, for in
this order there were few bishops and many presbyters (priests), to the number of 300.   They had one
head, our Lord, but used different Masses and different rules."

On this clause Lanigan[*] remarks, " the author's
meaning is as clear as daylight. He tells us that
whereas a diversity of liturgies, &c. was introduced
after the times of the first class of Saints, no such
diversity existed during the period that it (the first
class) lasted."   Ussher, in reference to the diversity
of liturgies or Masses, says,[†] " Et *Missæ* quidem sive
publice liturgie unum et eumdem ritum *initio* a *Pa-
tricio* huc introductum, et a discipulis illius ipsius
observatum ille notat;" that is, " the author of the

---

[*] Eccl. Hist. vol. ii. p. 16.
[†] Religion of Ancient Irish, p. 916.

Catalogue observes that " *the Mass* and *rite of celebration which St. Patrick introduced* remained identically the same throughout the entire country during the time of the first order of Saints." This admission of Ussher places beyond all doubt that the Mass was celebrated by St. Patrick, as well as by Columbanus and their successors.

"The third order of Saints was of this sort; they were holy presbyters and a few bishops, a hundred in number, who inhabited desert places, and lived on herbs and water, and the alms of the faithful, and had no property of their own, and they had different rules and liturgies" (*Masses*). This third order continued till 664, and brings us near the close of the seventh century.

Hence we find, on the authority of ancient documents which cannot be gainsayed, that the Mass was introduced into this country by St. Patrick, and was celebrated by all the orders of Irish Saints for the first two hundred years after the death of our National Apostle.

Ussher being thus confronted with venerable records, the existence of which he could not ignore, was sadly perplexed. To deny that the Early Irish believed in the Mass was impossible; to assert that they did not believe the Body and Blood of the Lord

D

to be therein consecrated and administered to the
faithful, would be to show profound ignorance of
church history: he therefore was driven to the wall,
and in his despair raised the cry, that the Early Irish
received the Sacrament under both kinds, therefore,
were different in their belief and practice from the
Roman Catholics of the present day. He undertakes
to prove this by extracts, which we subjoin.*

" Bede relates that one Hildmer, an officer of Eg-
frid, king of Northumberland, entreated our Cuthbert
to send a priest that might minister the Sacraments
of the Lord's Body and Blood unto his wife, who
was then dying. And Cuthbert himself immediately
before his own death, received the Communion of
the Lord's Body and Blood, as Herefride, Abbot of
Lindisfarne (who was the man that at that time administered the Sacrament to him), made report unto
the same Bede, who elsewhere, also, particularly
mentions that he there tasted of the cup,—' he tastes
the cup of life,' says he, 'and protects his upward
journey with the Blood of Christ.'" Ussher goes on
to say: "So we need not doubt what is meant by
that which we read in the book of the life of Saint
Fursæus, which was written before the time of Bede,
'that he received the Communion of the holy Body

* Religion of Ancient Irish, c. iv. p. 37.

and Blood, and that he wished to admonish the pastors of the Church, that they should strengthen the souls of the faithful with the spiritual food of doctrine, and the participation of the holy Body and Blood.'"

These passages prove to demonstration that the Early Irish Christians' belief was, that they received the holy Body and Blood of the Lord at Communion —but, in the first place, they do not prove that the Blessed Sacrament was administered under both kinds—as when administered under either species, *both the Body and Blood* are received according to Catholic faith—and secondly, even if such a conclusion as Ussher infers could be legitimately drawn, it would prove just nothing at all, because it would refer to a matter of mere discipline, and not at all of faith, and would in no way interfere with the point at issue, namely, that the Early Irish Christians held the doctrine of the Blessed Eucharist being the Body and Blood of Jesus Christ, and that Mass was celebrated as the Sacrifice of that Body and Blood.

Hence we see that the doctrine and practice of the Irish monks and nuns, and the general faithful, from the age of St. Patrick, relative to the Mass and. the holy Eucharist, were precisely the same with those of the Catholic Church of to-day, and altogether at

variance with the teachings of modern Protestantism.
Is it not then a falsification of the plainest facts of
our history, to set forth this statement which occurs
in the Protestant Church History of Ireland, by Rev.
R. King?*—" The year 831 is a notable one in the
history of Christianity, as being that in which the
doctrine of Transubstantiation was first clearly laid
down, and published in the Church. This was done
by a monk, named Paschasius Radbert, in a treatise
concerning the Body and Blood of Christ, in which
he set forth: 1st. That after Consecration nothing
but the appearance of bread and wine remained.
2nd. That the Body of Christ, thus present, was the
same Body which was born of the virgin, suffered on
the cross, and was raised from the dead. This *new*
doctrine excited the astonishment of many." Why
—the extract made from the Ancient Treatise on the
Mass† contains the fullest and most powerful exposition of the Catholic doctrine on the subject; the
Antiphonary of Bangor, which was written fully 100
years before Mr. King's notable year of 831, proclaims it; the practice of the Irish monks and nuns
under the guidance of Columbkille and Bridget ex-
emplify it, and last of all the *identical Missal* used by

* Church Hist. vol. ii. p. 401.
† See p. 26, also MS. Materials of Irish Hist. p. 376.

Columbkille's great contemporary, St. Columbanus, is still in existence, and contains Masses said by the Fathers and founders of the Early Irish Christian Church. As we shall have occasion to refer at some length to this Missal, when treating of other points of Catholic doctrine, and that we have presented abundant evidence on this first point of our enquiry, to satisfy any honest reader, we now draw our legitimate conclusion, viz:—That the faith of the Early Irish Church on the Blessed Eucharist and the sacrifice of the Mass, was in every respect the same as that professed by the Irish Catholics of to-day.

CHAPTER II.

Section I.

ON THE POWER OF ABSOLVING FROM SIN EXERCISED IN THE SACRA-
MENT OF PENANCE, AND THE PRACTICE OF CONFESSION IN THE
EARLY IRISH CHURCH.

Ussher's* admissions remove all difficulty on this
point. He states that " upon *special* occasions they
(the Early Irish Christians) *did, no doubt,* both pub-
licly and *privately,* make confession of their faults,
as well that they might receive counsel and direction
for their recovery, as that they might be made par-
takers of the *benefit of the keys,* for the quieting of
their troubled conscience. . . . . *Sure we are* that this
was the practice of the ancient Scottish and Irish."
Is this the practice of modern Protestants? We
have yet to learn that it is. In the next page Ussher
continues, " One old penitential canon we find laid
down in a synod, held in this country about 450, A.D.,
by St. Patrick, Auxilius, and Isserninus, which is as
follows:—' A Christian who has committed murder,
or fornication, or gone to a soothsayer, after the
manner of the Gentiles, for every such crime shall

* Religion of Ancient Irish, chap. vi, p. 46.

do a year of penance; when his year of penance is accomplished, he shall come with witnesses, and afterwards he shall be *absolved by a priest.'*" With such concessions before us, it cannot be necessary to allege any further proofs. However, it may be interesting to allege a few examples. Domestic events do not constitute history, and hence the occurrences of every day pass unheeded, and are embodied in no permanent record. There are hundreds of priests engaged in hearing confessions, throughout each diocese in Ireland; but being a matter of every-day life in our Church, it forms no prominent topic in our annals. Only when a clergyman is placed in a conspicuous position—such as being appointed chaplain to a lord mayor, or confessor to some crowned head —do his duties assume such importance that they attract and receive public notice. Instances of this kind we meet with from the earliest Christian period in Ireland.

St. Domnan of Eigg suffered martyrdom on the 17th of April, 617. He was somewhat junior to Columbkille, in whose community he was enrolled. Dr. Reeves* quotes from the festology of Ængus, a work of the eighth century: " This Domnan went to Columbkille to make him his *soul's friend*" (anmchara).

* Vita Columbæ, Notes, p. 305.

In a note on this word anmchara (soul's friend), Reeves adds, "Anmchara is the term commonly used in Irish records to denote *confessarius*." Here, then, we have a work of undoubted genuineness, belonging to the eighth century, recording of St. Domnan, who lived in the sixth and seventh centuries, that he chose as his confessor, his friend St. Columbkille; and the special word used in early Irish history to designate the confessor or soul's friend, is pointed out by the learned antiquary Dr. Reeves.

Another instance is recorded[*] in the Summary of St. Columbkille's life, by the last-named author.

"Conall, the lord of Dalriada," (present Co. Antrim) " died in 574; whereupon, his cousin Aidan assumed the sovereignty, and was formally inaugurated by St. Columba, in the monastery of Hy..... Irish writers," adds Dr. Reeves, "style St. Columba 'the anmchara,' that is, soul's friend, or *confessarius* of king Aidan."

In the life of St. Fintan[†] we read, that he was recommended by St. Columba, as *confessor* to a young religious named Columbanus: many similar cases are recorded in our history[‡] One other extract will suffice to close this branch of the subject. It consists of a passage taken from a very interesting

* Vita Columbæ, p. lxxvi.
† Life of St. Fintan, c. xxii. quoted by Lanigan, vol. ii. p. 229.
‡ MS. Materials, O'Curry, p. 333.

document, entitled the "Litany of St. Ængus." The
authenticity of this Litany is admitted by Sir James
Ware, Petrie, Reeves, and King. It was composed,
O'Curry* informs us, about the year 798. The
Litany, in which are invoked a vast number of foreign
Saints buried in Ireland, begins thus:—

" The three-times fifty Roman pilgrims who settled
in Ui Melé...... invoco in auxilium meum, per
Jesum Christum ..... The 3,000 *father confessors*
who congregated in Munster to consider one question,
under Bishop Ibar ..... invoco in auxilium meum
per Jesum Christum." From this quotation it is
manifest that confession was not only practised, as
Ussher says, " upon special occasions," by the Early
Irish Christians, but throughout the entire country,
as a general and common exercise of religion. The
total number of Catholic clergy at present in Ireland
is about 3,000. These figures include both seculars
and regulars. If a convocation of all the priests in
Ireland were announced, it would be extremely difficult, even in those days of rapid and easy transition,
to assemble 2,000. Some would be prevented by old
age and infirmities, others should remain to attend the
sick, and discharge parochial duties. Hence it appears
that the confessors must have been more numerous

* MS. Materials of Irish Hist. p. 380.

in Ireland *in the sixth and seventh centuries*, than they are in the nineteenth, and, therefore, confession was then a general practice of the faithful as it is to-day.* We have referred the authority of the litany not merely to the eighth but even to the sixth century; for Dr. Petrie informs us that the invocations were in use at that early period:† "Of the great extent of the influx of foreigners to Ireland we have abundant testimony in the ancient litany used in Ireland in the sixth and seventh centuries, as preserved by St. Ængus, in which the holy foreigners interred in Ireland are invoked."

SECTION II.

PRAYERS FOR THE DEAD.—PURGATORY.

We shall now digress a little, in order to make the acquaintance of one of the greatest saints of old Ireland. St. Columbkille spent his early life, until he was forty years of age, in this country. He then retired to the island of Hy, or Iona, where he founded a monastery, and passed the remainder of his life, except during an occasional visit to Ireland, or the neighbouring coast of Scotland. When Columbkille was a young man of about twenty years, Columbanus was

---

* Several other instances may be seen in the Rev. J. O'Hanlon's learned Life of St. Malachy, p. 17.

† Dublin Penny Journal, vol. i. p. 98.

born in some part of Leinster.* He was destined to rival the illustrious fame of Columbkille. As he grew up to manhood he also became a monk, and devoted himself to study, at first in an island of Lough Erne, and afterwards under St. Comgall in the celebrated Monastery of Bangor, county Down. When about fifty years old, he set out, accompanied by twelve other monks, on a foreign mission. He established three monasteries in the west of France. He subsequently preached the Gospel in Germany and Switzerland, where he left after him one of his companions, St. Gall, who founded a monastery which gives its name to a town and canton in Switzerland. To the eloquent pen of Montalembert the Catholic world is indebted for a graphic history of St. Columbanus.† After leaving Switzerland the Saint crossed the mountains into Italy, and there, in a gorge of the Appenines, established the Monastery of Bobbio. It contained the best library in Europe in the middle ages, and flourished for 1,100 years, till suppressed by the French in the revolutions of the last century. One of the books of its library, still preserved, and now deposited in the Ambrosian Library, at Milan, is the Missal or Mass-book of Columbanus, to which

* The precise year of his birth is not known.　Lanigan and King consider 539 the most probable date.

† Monks of the West, vol. ii.

reference has been already made.   Mahillon, the learned Benedictine, discovered this Missal at Bobbio; and as he testifies that it was in his time (the seventeenth century) at least 1,000 years old, this brings its date back to the age of Columbanus.   It is so extremely interesting a memorial of the ancient Irish Church, that we subjoin the description given of it by Dr. Lanigan.*—"From its antiquity, it is clear that it must have been brought to Bobbio by Saint Columbanus or some of his disciples; and hence arises a strong presumption that it was the liturgy used by him.   The part of the Mass called *the Canon*, is taken from that of the Roman liturgy, and agrees nearly with it as it is read at present;† yet it has in the article 'Communicantes,' after Cosmæ et Damianæ, the names of some other saints, among whom is Saint Martin.   In this Missal there are few Masses for saints.   It has those for Saint Stephen, the apostles James and John, the Cathedra Sti. Petri, the Assumption of the B. Virgin, the Finding of the holy Cross, the Nativity of St. John the Baptist, and his Passion, Saints Peter and Paul, the king Sigismund, Saint

---

* Eccl. Hist. vol. iv. p. 372.

† This statement is most important, as the words of consecration—"This is my Body," &c.—"This is the Blood of the New Testament," &c., by which the change of the bread and wine into the Body and Blood of Christ is effected by the power of God, occur in the *Canon*.

Martin of Tours, and Michael the Archangel. It
has three Rogations before the Ascension, and *two
Masses for the dead,* one in general, and another
Missa sacerdotis defuncti. . . . . . The antiquity of
this Missal appears from the wording of the Creed,
which we find in it; for although it is the same in substance as the Roman Creed, commonly called the
Apostles' Creed, yet several words are different. To
show that the copy found at Bobbio was written in
Ireland, or at least by an Irishman, it is asserted that
the characters or letters are exactly of the same kind
as those of ancient manuscripts recognised to have
been written by Irishmen.* Add, that as is usual in
such old manuscripts, certain vowels and consonants
are frequently interchanged for each other, according
to a mode peculiar to the Irish, and that some eminent
diplomatists think it probable that St. Columbanus
brought that Missal from his own country. On the
whole, although I do not pretend to decide on the
matter, I cannot but think that said Missal was the
one used by that saint himself, and that the only difference between it and the ancient Cursus Scotorum,
consists in his having added to it the Mass of St.

* The peculiarity of the Irish school in the formation and illumination of the capital letters, is easily recognized by any one
conversant with Irish manuscripts. See Digby Wyatt's Art of
Illuminating, for illustrations of the ancient Irish manuscripts.

Sigismund, in compliance with the custom of the province of Besançon."

That this Missal was the one actually used by St. Columbanus, a few hypercritics may affect to disbelieve. It is sufficient for our purpose to know that it is an Irish Missal of the time of the saint, viz., the seventh century. The Masses contained in this precious relic of by-gone ages, prove at once convincingly that the Irish Church of the seventh century—1st. Prayed for the dead, and offered the Holy Sacrifice for their eternal repose. 2ndly. Practised devotion to the Blessed Virgin, and celebrated, as a solemn festival, the feast of her Assumption into heaven. 3rdly. Invoked the saints, in whose honor special Masses were offered. 4thly. Venerated sacred relics, and especially *the cross*; "the finding" of which was consecrated by a particular Mass, as it is at this present time on the 3rd of May. And 5thly. Showed its reverence for the Chair of St. Peter, as we now set aside the 18th of January for "the Feast of the Chair" of the prince of the Apostles.

Ussher denies that these prayers for the dead and "requiem" Masses had anything to do with the doctrine of purgatory, because, he alleges, they were offered not as a propitiation, but as a thanksgiving. His words are—" Neither the commemoration, nor the praying for the dead, nor the Requiem Masses (all of which he admits as then practised), has any necessary relation to Purgatory, because they were merely thanksgiving." This subterfuge of Ussher is exposed by an example quoted by himself.* "Magnus said, on his death-bed, to his friend Tozzo, bishop of Ausboro, 'Do not weep because thou beholdest me labouring in so many storms of worldly troubles, because I believe in the mercy of God that my soul shall rejoice in the freedom of immortality; yet I beseech thee that thou *wilt not cease* to help me, a sinner, and my soul, with thy holy prayers.'" As Magnus was then dying, the continuous assistance he solicited was clearly to be given him after his death.

Again, the prayers of the requiem Masses which were then in use, put the matter beyond all question. The Penitential of Cummian, written in the seventh century, refers to these requiem Masses; and in the Missal found in Bobbio, which we have already described, are contained various prayers to God for *the pardon of the deceased*, and for the remission of their sins. Thus, in a Mass for the dead, entitled "Pro Defunctis," these words occur—"Tribuas ei (famulo tuo defuncto) Domine, delictorum suorum veniam, in illo secreto receptaculo, ubi jam non est

* Religion of Ancient Irish, p. 28.

locus penitentiæ. Tu, autem, Christé, recipe animam
famuli tui illo quam dedisti, et dimitte ejus debita
magis quam ille dimisit debitoribus suis."—" Grant, O
Lord, to your deceased servant, the *pardon of his sins*
in that secret receptacle where there is no opportunity
of doing penance. And do thou, O Christ, receive
the soul of thy servant, and *pardon* his *offences* more
fully than he forgave those who offended him."

And in a Mass for both living and dead—" Pro
vivis et defunctis," we read in the first prayer—
" Concede propitius, ut hæc sacra oblatio mortuis
prosit ad veniam, et vivis proficiat ad salutem."—
" Mercifully grant that this sacred oblation may *procure pardon for the dead*, and may promote the salvation of the living."

No further proof of the practice of praying for
the dead can be desired. Yet before we leave this
subject, let us take a glance at the burial places of
the Early Christian Irish.

IRISH GRAVE-YARDS.

A visit to those hallowed depositaries of all that
remains of the sainted men and women who shed
lustre upon Ireland in the ages of her bygone glory,
at once proclaims the belief which was then professed
in Erin. The dust of the dead " who died in the

Lord" blends with mother earth under the shadow of the Irish cross,—whilst the simple inscription—" Pray for the deceased," bespeaks the abiding faith of the mourning survivors—

> " And though no friendly hand garland the cross
> Above my moss,
> Still will the dear, dear moon tenderly shine
> Down on that sign."

Innumerable instances might be cited. We shall content ourselves with a few.

St. Breccan founded the Monastery of Ardbraccan, in the County Meath, in the sixth or seventh century. He afterwards retired to the great island of Arran, in Galway Bay, and there settled for life. He was interred in a church which he founded in that island. Dr. Petrie* tells us that his tomb was discovered about forty years ago. Within the sepulchre there was also found on this occasion a small water-worn stone of black calp or limestone; on the upper side is carved a plain cross, and around this in a circle, the following simple inscription:—" A prayer for Breccan the pilgrim."

At Monasterboice, near Drogheda, are three large Irish crosses. Dr. Wilde, in his eloquent book on " the Boyne and Blackwater," says of them:†—" The

---

* Round Towers ; Vol. xx. Trans. R.I.A., p. 138-9.
† Boyne and Blackwater, p. 297, second edition.

most attractive objects of antiquity here are those
magnificently-sculptured crosses, which have been
not only the great boast of Irish antiquaries, but
which have so frequently, and in such glowing terms,
elicited the admiration of foreigners.   With the
exception of the great cross at Clonmacnoise, and one
which we ourselves recently exhumed near the
cathedral of St. Breccan in the great island of Arran,
there is nothing of the kind in Great Britain, or perhaps in Europe, either in magnitude, design, or
execution to compare with two at least of the crosses
at Monasterboice."   Wilde goes on to describe the
dimensions and sculpture of these crosses.   He tells
us that in the larger of the two celebrated crosses
"the various compartments contain figures of the
Apostles, *the Virgin and Child,* and some of our Irish
saints and most celebrated ecclesiastics."   He adds,
" inferior in point of size, but eminently superior in
artistic design and execution, is the second crucial
monument, which we know, from an Irish inscription
on its base, was erected by Abbot Muiredach—' A
prayer for Muiredach, by whom this cross was made.' "
As there were only two distinguished abbots of this
name, one of whom died in 844, and the other in
924, the cross must be the work of the ninth or at
latest the tenth century.

CLONMACNOISE.—The waters of Ireland's noblest river, the Shannon, flow silently and solemnly, as if conscious of the sacred character of the place around Clonmacnoise, the burial-ground for more than a thousand years of the kings and nobles of Meath and Connaught. Here St. Kiaran founded a monastery in 547 or 548.* Devoted men collected around him, and spent their lives in the practice of exalted virtue and the pursuit of varied learning. Professors representing every branch of knowledge lectured to crowded audiences of students, assembled not only from various parts of Ireland, but from many of the countries on the continent. Thus centuries rolled over this quiet retreat of sanctity and learning, till the despoiler came to plunder the homes, and profane the sanctuaries, and confiscate the property of the peaceful recluses. The lonely round tower, the ruined chancel, and the broken and scattered fragments of moss-covered tombstones,—all speak of decay and desolation.

In 924 died Colman, abbot of Clonard and Clonmacnoise. This learned bishop erected the great cross of Clonmacnoise, to which Wilde refers as equal in beauty of outline and splendour of execution to the crosses of Monasterboice. What a contrast to

* Annals of Four Masters, vol. i. p. 185.

the profane exhibition of vanity exhibited on modern monuments, is supplied by the few words relative to the dead, engraved on these Christian memorials!—

" A prayer for Colman, who made this cross on the King Flanu.
A prayer for Flann, son of Maelsechlain."

The Tuam cross was erected in the earlier part of the twelfth century. From the magnificent work of O'Neill, on " Irish Crosses," we learn that the inscriptions on the one at Tuam are—

" A prayer for Turlock O'Connor, for the Abbot of Jarlath, by whom was made this cross.
A prayer for O'Ossin, for the Abbot by whom it was made.
A prayer for the successor of Jarlath, for Aed O'Ossin, by whom was made this cross."

Dr. Petrie, in his " Round Towers," informs us[*] that " the usual practice appears to have been to mark the grave of Christians simply by unsquared flag-stones, marked with a cross." And in another place[†] he says—" There is scarcely a variety of cross which is not to be found as a typical ornament in our most ancient manuscripts, even in those of the sixth century, as well as on our ancient sepulchral monuments."

The Book of Kells, belonging to the sixth century, abounds with crosses. In the representation of the

* Trans. R. I. A. vol. xx. p. 450.
† Ibid. p. 227.

Virgin and Child there is a " glory" round the head
of the Mother of God which contains three crosses,
as Westwood remarks. The same author also observes that " the controversy of Christ, who is here
figured with a cruciferous nimbus similar to that of
the Virgin (above referred to), and the devil (Luke,
iv.), is represented in a most extraordinary drawing.
. . . . The four evangelical symbols are again
represented at the beginning of St. John's gospel
. . . . and the following leaf bears the portrait
of St. John." In this portrait St. John is represented
holding the stylus or pen in his right hand, and in
his left a copy of his gospels, with the cross on the
centre of the cover, just as it is to be found on our
Breviaries.

Thus we learn on authority above suspicion, that
the characteristics of the Irish grave-yards were the
sign of the cross and prayers for the dead. It is no
difficult matter to say to what Church such unequi-
vocal marks belong, as they are to be met with, not
in Mount Jerome, where the remains of Protestants
are interred, but upon every monument in Glasnevin
are they to be found to-day as they were a thousand
years ago in Monasterboice, Tuam, Kells, Clonmacnoise, and the other Christian grave-yards of old
Ireland.

Section III.

CONSTANT USE OF THE SIGN OF THE CROSS.—MIRACLES.

It is a strange result of difference of belief between professing Christians, that one Church should be distinguished from another by the use of the sign of the cross, the badge of our common redemption. Yet no one point of dissimilarity is more marked between Catholics and Protestants than their ideas and feelings with regard to the symbol of our salvation, whether it is brought under our notice in the permanent material of stone, or in the transient formation of it in the form of blessing ourselves before or after prayer. Sometimes enlightened clergymen of the Protestant Church venture to place the cross on the external of their church; but it is regarded with manifest disfavour, is considered as evidencing a disposition to Romanism, and generally will not be tolerated. This is too notorious to need any proof. Two recent illustrations show that the iconoclastic spirit is neither dead nor sleepeth. We read in the *Irish Times* of December 8th, 1862, that "the new Archbishop of York, Dr. Thomson, has shown a decided objection to Puseyite ornamentation in churches. On Friday week he objected to consecrate a church at Selsby Hill, near Stroud, until a floral cross had been removed from the altar." In this respect the feeling is quite the same in Ireland. In the *Freeman's Journal* of May 25, 1863, appeared a letter from Enniskerry relative to an outrage upon the church built there for the Protestants by the Marchioness of Londonderry. As that lady has recently become a Catholic, the ornamentation of the church became an object of hatred. " The cross," says the letter referred to, " that surmounts the church, was held to be quite an abomination, the beautiful stained glass windows became idolatrous and damnable, and the piety of the Protestants of Enniskerry could no longer tolerate them. Accordingly, on the occasion of Lord Powerscourt's late visit, a deputation of the most religious and godly of the parishioners waited on him to request that he would remove the cross and the stained glass windows."

A still more painful instance occurred during the rebellion of '98 in Kells, county Meath, which is thus alluded to by Wilde*—" Another fact connected with this cross (market cross of Kells), still keenly remembered by the inhabitants of Kells, is that it formed part of the gallows from which several men were hanged in 1798." In marked contrast to this feeling of aversion and profanation towards the sign

* Boyne and Blackwater, p. 148.

of our redemption, we have seen that the Irish cross was everywhere erected in our ancient grave-yards. Dr. Reeves * in reference to this subject observes that, " the sign of the cross was very generally employed as a *signum salutare.* Hence it was customary before milking to *cross* the pail, before tools were used to cross them ...... Hence the readiness to erect the substantial *vexillum crucis* on the site of any remarkable occurrence,—a tendency which got full credit for its development, when Hy was celebrated for her 360 crosses; for though the number is undoubtedly an exaggeration, yet it shows how very numerous the crosses in Hy must have been." So far for the practices of St. Columbkille and his monks.

The Rev. R. King† says of St. Columbanus's monks —" Some of their observances were less edifying, and savoured more of superstition, such as the constant use of the sign of the cross, with which they were accustomed to mark their vessels, spoons, lamps, etc., previously to using them, and which they employed also on various other occasions."

An interesting anecdote relative to the use of the sign of the cross is recorded in the life of St. Columb-

---

* Vita Columbæ, Notes, p. 351.
† Church Hist. vol. i. p. 287.

kille.* That saint retired with twelve companions from Ireland to Hy in 563. Having spent two years in founding a monastery and church in the island, he set about the work of converting the Picts, and was the first Christian missioner who appeared in that country. The King Brude, who was aware of his arrival, was determined not to admit him to his palace, and accordingly gave orders for the closing of the gates. The saint, nothing daunted, advanced to the gates, and made upon them the sign of the cross, whereupon he at once easily opened them with his own hands. Even if the reader be so sceptical as not to admit the miracle, yet the record of it by Adamnan, shows what was the belief in the efficacy of the sign of the cross entertained by St. Columb-kille's immediate followers.

The continuance of miraculous powers in the Church after the Apostolic age is denied, and the belief of such agency ridiculed by Protestants. How very different was the opinion of the Early Irish Church on this point, is abundantly demonstrated, first by Adamnan's life of St. Columba, and secondly by the life of St. Martin of Tours, both of which are filled with records of prodigies supernaturally worked by these two great servants of God. Adamnan in-

* See Adamnan, book ii. chap. 35.

forms us* that on one occasion when wine could not
be procured for the celebration of Mass, St. Columba
changed water into wine, and presented it for the
Holy Sacrifice. Adamnan states that this was the
first miracle wrought by our saint, as a similar one
was the first effected by our divine Redeemer, at
the marriage feast of Cana of Galilee. Adamnan
devotes an entire book, consisting of eighty-three
quarto pages, to record the miracles of the saint.
Amongst these are producing water from a rock,
calming a storm at sea, raising the dead to life, etc.
After recounting various prodigies worked by the
saint, Adamnan concludes thus†—" Here the second
book, which treats of miracles, is brought to a close;
yet, the reader is to observe that many well-attested
miracles are omitted lest the reader should be fatigued
by their recital." Now, is this like a record that
would emanate from any Protestant? The idea is
simply an absurdity. It is manifestly a chronicle of
Catholic minds and hands. The late Dr. Kelly, of
Maynooth, in an able article on the Church of St.
Patrick (*Dublin Review*, June, 1846), observes—" In
the celebrated book of Armagh, the book of St.
Patrick's own cathedral, and partly copied from his
own autograph volume, we have, together with some

* Life of St. Columba, p. 103.   † page 187.

copies of the Scripture, a copy of the Life of St.
Martin of Tours, by the Christian Sallust, Sulpicius
Severus, and letters on the same subject by the same
classic hand. We can judge of the reverence in
which this life was held from the fact of its being
treasured up with the sacred Scriptures, and committed to the guardianship of an hereditary keeper,
who had the revenue of eight townlands allotted for
his support. Open any chapter you please in that
life and miracles appear."—Christ and the angels
appear to St. Martin, c. iv. St. Martin flying from
Milan meets the evil one, c. iv. St. Martin raises to
life the dead catechumen, who tells on his return to
this world, that when the judge was going to pro-
nounce sentence, two angels presented the prayers
of St. Martin on his behalf, c. v. St. Martin orders
a pine-tree to be cut down, because it was an object
of idolatrous worship, but the tree is falling on himself until he makes the sign of the cross and turns it
the other way, c. x. What need of more. " Cura-
tionum nero, tam potens in eo gratia erat, ut nullus
fere ab eo ægrotus accesserit qui non continuo
reciperet sanitatem, c. xiv. Constat autem angelos
ab eo plerumque visos, c. xxiv."

CHAPTER III.

Section I.

VENERATION for the Saints in heaven, and the practice of asking their prayers, including a special reverence for the Mother of God,—these are admittedly
points of Catholic doctrine, and are sternly condemned by every form of Protestantism.   Let us
see what the Early Christian Church of Ireland held
relative to such disputed dogmas.   We have already
alluded to the litany of St. Ængus, a genuine composition of the eighth century, embodying the prayers
said by the Irish in the sixth and seventh centuries.
" The piety of Ængus," says Rev. R. King,* " is
such as can meet with little sympathy in the mind of
a well-instructed and enlightened Christian; for the
most striking and remarkable point in those litanies
is the circumstance, that they comprise numerous invocations addressed to a vast number of dead saints."
The litanies are not merely illustrative of the piety
of Ængus, but of the belief of the Christian Church
before and during his time.   They begin thus:—
" The three times fifty Roman pilgrims who settled

* Church Hist. vol. i. p. 355.

in Ui-Mele, etc.—Invoco in auxilium meum per Jesum Christum. The 3,000 father confessors who congregated in Munster to consider one question,—Invoco in auxilium meum per Jesum Christum. The other thrice fifty pilgrims of the men of Rome and Latium, who went into Scotland,—Invoco in auxilium meum per Jesum Christum. The thrice fifty Gaedhils of Erinn in holy orders, each of them a man of strict rule, who went in one body into pilgrimage, under Abban, the son of Ua Cormaic.—Invoco in auxilium meum per Jesum Christum."*

Westwood, in his celebrated work entitled Palæographia Sacra, gives a lengthened account of the Book of Kells: we extract the following:—" Ireland may justly be proud of the Book of Kells. This copy of the Gospels, traditionally asserted to have belonged to St. Columba, is unquestionably the most elaborately executed manuscript of early art now in existence; far excelling, in the gigantic size of the letters in the frontispieces of the Gospel, the excessive minuteness of the ornamental details, the number of its decorations, the fineness of the writing, and the endless variety of initial capital letters, with which every page is ornamented, the famous Gospel of Lindisfarne in the Cotonian library." As that

* MS. of Irish Hist. p. 381.

monastery was founded by Irish monks from Iona,
the glories of the Gospel of Lindisfarne belong to
Ireland. Westwood goes on to say—" The verso of
fol. 7, contains the drawing of the Virgin and
Child, copied in plate 1, which is inclosed within a
highly elaborate border composed of interlined
lacertine animals with dogs' heads. This singular
composition is interesting from the proof it affords
of the veneration of the Virgin Mary in the Early
Irish Church; the large size in which she is represented, as well as the glory round her head (which
singularly bears three small crosses) evidently indi-
cating the high respect with which the Mother of
Christ was regarded." Such testimony from this
learned English Protestant, thoroughly conversant
with ancient Irish manuscripts, places the special
veneration of the Early Christian Irish for the holy
Virgin beyond all contradiction.

In addition to the very interesting litany of
Ængus, which is described at length by O'Curry, we
have one still more dear to us, and equally ancient;
it is the Litany of the Blessed Virgin, which is preserved in the " Leabhar Mor," and deposited in the
Royal Irish Academy. In reference to it O'Curry*
says :—" The third piece of this fifth class is a

* MS. of Irish Hist. p. 380.

beautiful and ancient litany of the B.V.M., differing in many ways from her litany in other languages, and clearly showing that although it may be an imitation, it is not a translation. I believe it to be as old at least as the middle of the eighth century. It consists of fifty-nine invocations, beginning: O great Mary! O Mary greatest of all Marys! O greatest of women! O Queen of the Angels! etc., and it concludes with a beautiful and eloquent entreaty that she will lay the unworthy prayers, sighs, and groans of the sinners before her own merciful Son, *backed by her own all-powerful advocacy*, for the forgiveness of their sins."

The Most Rev. Dr. Cullen, in his pastoral on the Immaculate Conception* supplies us with a more lengthened extract from this beautiful old Irish litany.—"O great Mary! the greatest of woman-kind! O Queen of Angels! O Woman full and over-flowing with the grace of the holy Spirit! O blessed and ever-blessed Mother of Eternal Glory! Mother of the Church heavenly and earthly! Mother of love and forgiveness! Mother of golden effulgence! O honour of the sky! Sign of tranquillity! O door of heaven! O golden ark! O beauty of the virgins! Lady of the tribes! Fountain of the gardens! Cleansing of sins! O Mother of orphans! Breast of the

* Date of Pastoral, 8th December, 1862.

infant! Consolation of the poor! Star of the Ocean!
Mother of Christ! Comeliness as of the moon! Excellence as of the sun! O canceller of the reproach
of Eve! O Renewer of life! Beauty of womankind!
Head of the virgins! Enclosed garden! True fountain of greenness! Mother of God! O eternal virgin!
O royal throne of the Deity! Sanctuary of the holy
Spirit! Virgin of the stem of Jesse! Cedar of Leba-
non! Cypress of Sion! Crimson rose of the land of
Jacob! O effulgence of Nazareth! O glory of Jerusalem! O beauty of the world! O noblest in descent
of the Christian flock! O Queen of life! O ladder of
heaven! hear the prayer of the poor; spurn not the
ulcers and moans of the wretched. Let our devotions
and our aspirations be presented to the Creator by
thee; for we ourselves are not worthy of being heard
through our demerits. O powerful Lady of heaven
and earth! cancel our crimes, obliterate the stains of
our wickedness. For mercy sake suffer us not to be
carried away from thee as a prey by our enemies;
suffer not our souls to be condemned, and take us to
thyself for ever under thy protection."

Upon these sentences his Grace remarks:—" Such
were the glowing strains in which the Church of Ireland, in early times, delighted to depict the glories of
the Queen of Heaven. How different is the language

in which she is greeted by those who call themselves
followers of the Reformation, and who appear to
take a pride in insulting the name of the Mother of
God! What a proof that they have nothing in common with the doctrine of the ancient Church of
Ireland!"

In the Antiphonary of Bangor, a manuscript of
the eighth century, the following prayer to S. Patrick
occurs, as part of the hymn of Secundinus in honor
of the saint:—

> Patricius Episcopus, oret pro nobis omnibus,
> Ut deleantur protimus, peccata quæ commissimus.
>
> Patrick, bishop, pray for all of us,
> That our sins may be completely wiped away.

Dr. Todd tells us* that "we can scarcely doubt
the truth of the tradition, which ascribes this hymn
to a contemporary and disciple of St. Patrick. We
are distinctly told that the hymn was written in Dun-
shaughlin (Co. Meath), by St. Sechnall or Secundinus, and that this St. Sechnall was a nephew of St.
Patrick." It seems to have been written during the
life of St. Patrick, and it continued to be recited in
the Church for ages after his death, especially the
three last verses, namely:—

* Liber Hymnorum, p. 34.

F

In memoria æterna erit justus,
Ab auditione mala non timebit,
Patricii laudes semper dicamus
Ut nos cum illo defendat Deus.
Hibernenses omnes clamant ad te pueri,
Veni Sancti Patricii, salvos nos facere.

These quotations supply us with examples from the infancy of the Church in Ireland, of invoking the prayers of "the dead saints." Numberless other instances could be quoted. We shall content ourselves with a few.

In an ancient hymn in honor of St. Brigid, attributed, as Dr. Todd, informs us,[*] to St. Columbkille, or St. Ultan of Ardbreccan, this clause occurs:

" The perfect virgin, beloved, of sublime dignity,
I shall be saved at all times by my Leinster saint,"

that is, of course, by her prayers.

This hymn is a production of the seventh century (written, most likely, by St. Ultan of Ardbreccan, who died in 656). As the greatest encomium that can be conferred on St. Brigid, it compares her to the B.V.M.—" Nisi per istam virginem, Marie sancte similem." It concludes with a prayer invoking the intercession of the saint.[†]—" Brigida sancta, sedulo sit in nostro auxilio, ut mereamur coronam habere ac letitiam in conspectu angelorum in sæcula sæculo-

* Liber Hymnorum, p. 66.
† "St. Brigid, give us prompt assistance, that we may deserve to be for ever happy with the angels."

rum."* The editor goes on to say: "In a MS. called the Leabhar Breac (R.I.A.) there is a panegyric or life of St. Brigid. This piece, which from its language appears to be a production of not later than the tenth century, was obviously intended as a sort of sermon, to be read to the people on the feast of St. Brigid. It contains, amongst other praises of her innumerable virtues, the following:—" There was not in existence one of more bashfulness and modesty than this holy virgin. . . . . She was abstinent, unblemished, prayerful, patient, joying in the commandments of God; benevolent, humble, forgiving, charitable. She was a consecrated shrine for the preservation of the body of Christ. She was a temple of God;—*She is the Mary of the Irish.*"

In the festology of Ængus, the writer, as O'Curry tell us,† "beseeches Jesus, *through the intercession of his Mother*, to save him, as Jacob was saved from the hands of his brother," etc.

An important note of Dr. Todd's‡ will be read with much interest. He says that "there is an ancient copy of the Greek Psalter in Irish characters preserved in the library of Bâle. This remarkable

---

* Liber Hymnorum, p. 58.   † MS. Materials, p. 369.
‡ Liber Hymnorum, p. 55.

manuscript the editor (Dr. T.) had the privilege of examining in 1852. The Psalter cannot be of a later date than the ninth or tenth century; and the hymns written in the first few leaves are in an Irish hand, not later than the twelfth century. The first hymn begins—'Cantemus in omni die,' etc.; then follows a prayer to the B. V. Mary, beginning 'Singularis meriti, sola sine exemplo, mater et virgo Maria'; then follow two other hymns, then follows the verse 'Sancta virgo virginum Maria, intercede pro nobis.'* Over the words 'sancta virgo' in the same handwriting, occurs the word 'beatissima.' The above," adds the learned Doctor, "is probably a part of an ancient office, and it is curious that the epistle of our Lord to Abgarus (which comes immediately after the prayer to the B. Virgin) appears to have been used as a lesson, which is a singular proof of the antiquity of the office."

An ancient hymn, by St. Brogan of Cloen, is published in the Liber Hymnorum;†—one portion of it runs thus:

> "The veiled virgin, who drives over the Currech,
> Is a shield against sharp weapons—
> None was found her equal, except Mary:
> Let us put our trust in my strength."

* "Holy Mary, Virgin of virgins, pray for us."   † p. 67.

The hymn refers to St. Brigid, and Dr. Todd observes that in the last line there is a play upon the name of St. Brigid and the Irish word *brigi, strength*. In another part of the poem we read:

> " There are two virgins in heaven
> Who will not give me a forgetful protection,
> Mary, and Saint Brigid:
> Under the protection of them both may we remain.

We will draw our examples to a close with the Hymn of St. Cummian. He was bishop of Clonfert,[*] was born in 589 or 590, a few years before the death of Columbkille, and died in 661 or 662. He was a most learned ecclesiastic. His hymn contains an invocation in every verse of a particular saint, and an appeal to the prayers of each of the apostles, Paul, Andrew, James, John, etc., Matthew, Mark, and St. Patrick.[†] We shall give the reference to our national Apostle.

> 1. Patrici patris obsecremus merita
>   Ut Deo digna perpetremus opera.—Alleluia.
> 2. Horum sanctorum bina septem valida
>   Fiant pro nobis scutata suffragia.—Alleluia.
> 3. Quibus ignita dæmonumi jacula
>   Possunt extingui ut per propugnacula.—Alleluia.[‡]

In addition to the practice of invoking the Blessed

---

[*] Lanigan, vol. ii. p. 398.
[†] See more on this subject in O'Curry's MS. Mat., p. 379.
[‡] Liber Hymn. p. 78-9.

Virgin Mary, of which we have supplied abundant proofs, it was also the custom to dedicate abbeys and churches and oratories to her name, and in her honor. Dean Butler, in his learned though dry compilation, entitled Trim Castle,* commences his account of St. Mary's Abbey, with this admission—" Colgan informs us that so early as the year 432 St. Patrick founded this Abbey of Canons Regular, dedicated it to the Virgin Mary, and built it on a piece of ground given for that purpose by Fethlemid, the son of Leoghaire, and grandson of Niall."

Wilde has recorded the tradition as to the locality of this foundation of Mary's Abbey in these words†—" The original abbey, which was dedicated to the Virgin Mary, stood, in all probability, upon the picturesque site of the Yellow Tower, which in after ages was erected here, and is stated to be the most lofty remnant of Anglo-Norman architecture now existing in Ireland."

Archdall's Monasticon, under the head of Clonfert, has that‡ St. Brendan, the son of Findloga, studied under St. Finian, in the Academy of Clonard; and

* Trim Castle, p. 181.
† Boyne and Blackwater, p. 83.
‡ Monasticon, p. 278.

A.D. 553 or 562, he founded an abbey here, under the invocation of the Virgin Mary."

Again, Wilde* tells us of Kells, county Meath, that—" Dermod, the son of Fergus Kervail, made a grant of this place (Kells) to St. Columb, who founded a monastery here, about the year 550, and dedicated it to the Virgin Mary."

St. Columbanus likewise dedicated an oratory, which he erected at Bobbio, to the Mother of God, as we learn from Dr. Petrie†—" The oratories erected abroad by the Irish ecclesiastics were similar in size and material to those in their native country—as in the following example from the life of Columbanus," describing the oratory erected by him at Bobbio— " Ubi etiam ecclesiam in honorem almæ Dei genitricis, semperque virginis Mariæ, ex lignis construxit ad magnitudinem sanctissimi corporis sui."‡

In our convent schools, both in this and in every Catholic country, there is a badge of merit much coveted by the pupils. It consists of a blue riband worn only by those who are called the " children of Mary." It is a curious fact that we find in the early

---

* Boyne and Blackwater, p. 144.　　† Round Towers, p. 349.

‡ " Where he also constructed a wooden church in honor of the ever Virgin Mother of God," etc.

Irish annals the name "servant of Mary" as commonly used amongst the people. In the Annals of the Four Masters, occurs this entry—"A.D. 893. Maelmaire, son of Flanagan, died." Again—"A.D. 918. Maelmaire, Abbot of Ard-Breacain, died."* This word Maelmaire means " servant of Mary."

Again the famous annalist Marianus Scotus, who went from Ireland to Cologne, and afterwards removed to Metz, where he died in 1086, bore the same name, as Marianus (Scotus) is the latinized form of Maelmaire, servant of Mary, a name then common in Ireland. So says Haverty in his valuable history of Ireland.† Thus we find the records of Early Christian Ireland crowded with evidence of the practice of invoking the saints, and especially of appealing for assistance to the Blessed Virgin Mary. The Hymn of Secundinus, written by St. Patrick's nephew, the Book of Kells, the Litany of St. Ængus, embodying the prayers recited in the sixth and seventh centuries in Ireland, the Litany of the Blessed Virgin, as old at least as the eighth century, the Antiphonary of Bangor, the Hymn of St. Ultan

* Persons bearing the name "servant of Mary," are also recorded under the dates A.D. 951, 964, 994.—Annals Four Masters.
† Haverty's History, p. 155.

in honor of St. Brigid, as old as the age of St. Columbkille, the Festology of Ængus, the Greek Psalter in Irish characters in the library of Bâle,—all combine to attest this Catholic practice. Add to these proofs, the dedication of churches, abbeys, and oratories to the Blessed Virgin Mary, and the calling oneself "servant of Mary," and the weight of evidence thus presented becomes overwhelming for this point of Catholic doctrine and practice.

SECTION II.

ON FASTING.

WE pass on from the intercession of the saints, and the special reverence and devotion to the Mother of God, to consider the doctrine and practice of the Early Irish Church on fasting and mortification. Dr. Reeves[*] informs us that "in the exercise of fasting, the founder (St. Columbkille) is said to have shown continual diligence. Every Wednesday and Friday throughout the year was a fast day, except in the interval between Easter and Whitsunday, and no food was taken till the nona (3 o'clock, p.m.) unless

[*] Vita Columbæ, p. 348.

where the prior claims of hospitality demanded an exception to the rule. Lent was strictly kept as a preparation for Easter, and during this season the fast was prolonged every day, except Sunday, till evening, when a light meal, consisting of such food as bread, diluted milk, and eggs, was taken." Hence it appears that the Irish monks, besides two fast days every week, fasted every day in Lent, till evening, and took no meat whatsoever during the entire of that holy season. Had the monks been Protestants such would scarcely have been their practice—whilst in the simplicity and frugality of their meals, we recognise an exact description of the fasting fare of the Monks of Mount Melleray—" bread, diluted milk, and eggs." We should not feel much surprise if Mr. Whiteside shall ask us some fine day to believe that all the monks in Melleray belong to the Established Church !

The monastic rule of Columbanus is precisely similar. The Rev. Mr. King* thus translates it— " The monk's food is to be of an humble quality, and taken towards evening, avoiding satiety and excess of drink, that it may support and not hurt them.

* Church Hist. vol. i. p. 282. The original is contained in Fleming's Collectanea.

Let it be vegetables, pulse, meal mixed with water, with a little biscuit. Therefore, fasting is to be practised every day, as well as the use of refreshments every day, and while food is to be taken every day, the indulgence allowed to the body should at the same time be of an humble and sparing character, because our daily eating is with a view to our daily improving, daily praying, daily labouring and daily reading."

On this rule Mr. King remarks—"The abstaining from food until evening appears not to have been very strictly observed or enjoined, except on Wednesdays or Fridays. With respect to these two days, the rule of penances enacted, that "if any one were to eat," on them "before the ninth hour, (*i.e.* before three o'clock) 'unless he were weak,'" he should fast for two days on "bread and water." On ordinary occasions fish was sometimes used by the followers of Columbanus; but they and the old monks of Ireland, generally appear to have abstained from flesh meat, although they used to treat their guests and strangers to it."

That Columbanus set an example of great mortification and abstinence to his disciples for whom he made such rules, will appear from the following

passage which occurs in his life by Jonas.* The
eighth chapter is headed "De mira ejus abstinentia.—
Erat cibus ejus ita attenuatus ut vix eum vivere
crederes, nec aliud penitus quam agrestium herbarum
exigua mensura, vel pomorum parvulorum; potus
aqua erat" etc. "On his extraordinary abstinence.—
His food was so scanty, that one can scarcely believe he could live upon such fare. It consisted of
a very small amount of herbs, a few apples; his
drink was water," etc.

Thus we see it acknowledged by unquestionable
witnesses, and clearly set forth in the most venerable
of our Christian records, that the teaching and practice of our Early Church upheld the anti-Protestant
doctrine of fasting and mortification.

* Jonas' Life, c. 8.

CHAPTER IV.

THE SUPREMACY OF THE POPE.

WE come now to the spot upon which Protestants
take their last stand, viz:—The independence of the
Early Christian Church in Ireland from all allegiance
to the See of Rome. "As true," says Wilde,* "as
that the Irish people were governed by their own
kings and princes, and were amenable to their own
laws and brehons only, up to the middle of the
twelfth century, so true is it that the Irish Catholic
Church was independent of all foreign rule, in either
temporal or spiritual matters, until the beginning of
that period." We have nothing to say to the temporal
dominion of the Pope over this country. The question for us to decide is—Did the Early Irish Church
acknowledge the supremacy of the Pope or reject it?
We affirm that Church did submit to the jurisdiction
of Rome, for the following reasons: 1. The Irish
Christian Church was founded by the Church of

* Boyne and Blackwater, p. 281.

Rome, and was a daughter of that Church. 2. From the earliest ages of Christianity in this country, it was the custom of the Irish Church to consult the Holy See in its difficulties, to appeal to that See as supreme judge, and to be guided by its decisions. We shall endeavour to prove these two points beyond all cavil.

First, then, we ask—Who founded the Irish Christian Church? The first Christian bishop who ever set foot in Ireland arrived here in 431. His name was Palladius; his mission was unsuccessful; he left the country in the same year, and retired to Scotland, where he died in a short time. He was succeeded by St. Patrick, who was sent from Rome, as Palladius had also been, to convert the country from Paganism. This mission from the Holy See, of both Palladius and St. Patrick, is distinctly admitted by Ussher*—"From the first legation of Palladius and Patricius, *who were sent to plant the faith* in this country—it cannot be showed out of any monument of antiquity, that the Bishop of Rome ever sent any of his legates before Gillebertus," etc. Some modern Protestant writers affirm that Ussher admitted too easily the mission of St. Patrick from

---

* Religion of Ancient Irish, c. viii. p. 74.

Rome. Canon Wordsworth is one of this class. But the evidence to prove that Ussher could not deny it in the face of history, is abundant and conclusive.

1. Erric, of Auxerre, a French monk of the ninth century,* in his life of St. German of Auxerre, tells us that St. German sent Patrick to Rome, accompanied by a priest named Segetius, who carried with him recommendatory letters of Patrick, and that Pope Celestine, receiving such favourable testimony to Patrick's merits from St. German, gave him the Apostolical benediction, and sent him to preach the faith in Ireland. " Ad sanctum Celestinum urbis Romæ Papam per Segetium presbyterum suum eum direxit (Germanus) qui viro præstantissimo probitatis ecclesiasticæ testimonium apud sedem ferret apostolicam, cujus judicio approbatus, auctoritate fultus, benedictione denique roboratus, Hibernice partes expetiit."

2. Mark the Anchorite was a contemporary of Erric of Auxerre. In his history of the Britons, he tells us that Pope Celestine first sent Palladius to convert the Irish, and on his death, then dispatched St. Patrick on the same mission.—" Missus est Palla-

* Lanigan's Ecclesiastical History, vol. i. p. 193.

dius episcopus primus a Celestino Papa Romano ad
Scottos episcopo convertendos, et Palladius rediens
de Hibernia ad Brittanniam, ibi defunctus est in terra
Pictorum. Conscia autem morte Palladii episcopi, a
Celestino Papa Romano, et angelo Dei comitante,
monente atque adjuvante Victore, et a Germano episcopo ad Scottos ad fidem sanctæ Trinitatis convertendos Patricius missus est."* (Historia Britonum).
The same fact is testified by Nennius, in his history
of the Britons, by Marianus Scotus in his chronicle,
by Sigebert, the monk of Gemblours, and by St.
Columbanus in his letter to Pope Boniface, wherein
he says—" Nullus hereticus, nullus Judæus, nullus
schismaticus fuit, sed fides, sicut a vobis primum
sanctorum scilicet apostolorum successoribus tradita
est inconcussa tenetur," which is thus fairly rendered
by Rev. R. King.†—" There has been among us no
Jew, nor heretic, nor schismatic; but the Catholic faith
as it was delivered at the first by you, that is to say,
by the successors of the holy Apostles, is still maintained among us with unshaken fidelity." This testimony of Columbanus has peculiar force, as it occurs
in a very outspoken letter, to which Protestant writers

---

* See Rock's Letter to Lord J. Manners, p. 29.
† Hist. of the Church of Ireland, vol. iii. p. 942.

appeal to show that he did not submit to the authority of the pope. With that we shall deal by-and-by.

Many other authorities might be quoted, but we shall content ourselves by referring to William of Malmesbury, the Annals of Innisfallen, and the Annals of the Four Masters, all of which agree in stating that St. Patrick got his mission from Pope Celestine.* The Rev. Dr. William Todd, in a work entitled "The Church of St. Patrick," written by him before his conversion to Catholicity, undertook to show that the Irish Church did not acknowledge any allegiance to Rome; yet treating on this mission of St. Patrick, says†—"I am disposed to agree with those who hold that the Irish Church was founded by a pope "—if we are content to understand by these words that the Pope Celestine gave his sanction and blessing to the mission of St. Patrick, when that of Palladius had proved to be a failure." St. Cummian, in his celebrated epistle on the Paschal controversy, supplies this pointed illustration.—"We sent those whom we knew to be wise and humble men, as it were children to their mother, to Rome, to make inquiries concerning the time for keeping Easter." "Misimus quos

* Most of these authorities are quoted in Dr. Rock's Letter p. 31, &c.
† Church of St. Patrick, p. 26.

G

novimus sapientes et humiles esse, velut natos ad matrem, et ad Romam urbem aliqui ex eis venientes,"
etc.* From all these authorities we deduce our first
conclusion, as already stated—namely, that the Irish
Christian Church was founded by the Church of
Rome, and was a daughter of that Church.

2. We allege that this Church, so founded by
Pope Celestine, was accustomed from the very beginning of its existence to consult the Holy See in its
difficulties, to appeal to that see for its guidance,
and to be directed by its decisions; in one word, that
the Irish Church was placed, from its very infancy,
under the spiritual dominion of the Holy See.

This, we contend, is plain, from a council held by
St. Patrick, assisted by Benignus, Auxilius, and
Secundinus. Several canons for the government of
the Irish Church were drawn up at this synod. "One
of these," to which we have already referred, "is of
especial interest," says O'Curry,† " as it preserves to
us the most perfect evidence of the connection of the
Catholic Church in Erinn with the See of Rome,
from the very first introduction of Christianity into
the country." It is as follows:—" Moreover if any
case should arise of extreme difficulty, and beyond

* Quoted by Rock, p. 17.
† MS. Materials of Irish Hist. p. 372-3.

the knowledge of all the judges of the nations of the Scots,* it is to be duly referred to the chair of the Archbishop of the Gaedhil, that is to say, of Patrick, and the jurisdiction of this bishop (of Armagh). But if such a case as aforesaid, of a matter at issue, cannot be easily disposed of (by him) with his counsellors in that (investigation), *we have decreed* that it be sent to the Apostolic Seat, that is to say, to the Chair of the Apostle Peter, having the authority of the See of Rome." "These are the persons who decreed concerning this matter—namely, Auxilius, Patrick, Secundinus, and Benignus."† The original of the decree is given in Appendix No. 117 of O'Curry's invaluable work, so often quoted in these pages. Ussher knew not how to grapple with this formidable canon. His attempts to ward off the formidable blows dealt by it at his theory of "the Independence of the Early Irish Church" are ludicrous. He says—"that the Irish were wont to consult with the Bishop of Rome, when difficult questions arose, we easily grant; but that they thought they were bound in conscience to abide by his judgment . . . .

---

* Marianus Scotus, who died in 1086, was the first who applied the name *Scotia* to Scotland. It was previously known as Alba. The word Scots in the canon designated the Irish.

† Benignus succeeded St. Patrick in the See of Armagh.

is the point that we would fain see proved." Can
stronger proof be given than the command of this
synod?—" We have decreed that it be sent to the
Apostolic Seat, that is to say, to the Chair of the Apostle Peter, having the authority of the See of Rome."
Here we have the decree of St. Patrick, his immediate
successor St. Benignus, and the other bishops met with
them in solemn conclave, directing difficult questions
to be referred to Rome, which possessed the authority
to examine and finally adjudicate, as the supreme
court of appeal. Ussher in despair exclaims—" This
only I will say, that as it is most likely that St.
Patrick had a special regard to the Church of Rome,
from whence he was sent for the conversion of this
island, so if I myself had lived in his days, for the
resolution of a doubtful question, I should as willingly
have listened to the judgment of the Church of
Rome, as to the determination of any church in the
whole world; so reverend an estimation have I of the
integrity of that Church as it stood in those days."
Poor Ussher must have been in the last extremity
before he penned that admission, forced from him by
the crushing weight of historical evidence. It is the
custom of many Protestant writers to assert that the
Church became corrupt after the first three centuries.
Yet here Ussher speaks of the Church of Rome in

the close of the fifth century, as one of the purest in the world.

Dr. Lanigan's remarks upon the decree of this Synod of St. Patrick are worthy of note. He says*—" these canons prove, besides the primacy of Armagh, that the Irish Church did from the beginning acknowledge the supremacy of the See of Rome ; otherwise, would it have referred its difficult questions to a see so distant from Ireland, while at that period there were several eminent churches much nearer to us, such as those of Tours, Toledo, etc.—unless a peculiar prerogative were believed to belong to the Chair of St. Peter."

Canon Wordsworth's attempt to prove that St. Patrick was not sent from Rome is scarcely worth refuting. He says that neither Prosper Aquitanus, nor Bede make mention of such a mission. But assuredly a negative argument of that kind is of no value when opposed to the many authorities we have already quoted which possitively assert the mission, and call Rome the mother of the Irish Church. In his third sermon, the worthy canon treats us to an illustration about discovering the source of the Nile, which is so puerile that he penned it most probably

* Eccl. Hist. vol ii. p. 391.

as an amusing joke. He goes on to say—
" We have found that the stream of Papal power is
not visible in the centuries through which we have
passed. We now approach the spot in which it takes
its rise. We see it emerging from the earth. We
can point to the source of the Nile; hence we are
sure that our previous researches were correct. We
see the Church of Ireland enslaved at a particular
period; hence we know that before that time it was
free. The novelty of Papal domination, and the antiquity of Irish independence, is thus proved beyond
the power of contradiction, and the argument is complete. In the ninth century after Christ, Ireland
was invaded by the Danes,"* etc. Of course the
stream of Papal power is not visible to him, or to
any man that shuts his eyes deliberately lest he should
see. Has the doctor read Irish history? Has he
never heard of the Canon of St. Patrick, decreeing
all difficult questions to be sent to Rome for adjudication? Is he aware of the Synod of Old Leighlin,
and its ratifying and acting upon the Canon of St.
Patrick, by sending a deputation to Rome? Dr.
Wordsworth must really have been away on the

* We make these quotations from a work entitled "Good News
from Ireland," which contains a glowing account of imaginary con-
versions, put together with the avowed object of raising money.

banks of the Nile looking for its source, when he imagined he was studying our ancient records. Dr. Todd in his Church of St. Patrick admits that "these canons (viz. directing difficult questions to be referred to Rome) were in all probability enacted by the Church in Ireland some time between the fifth and eight century."[*]

The ignorance or misrepresentation of Canon Wordsworth in matters of Irish history will appear from the fact that he traces the spread of monastic houses in Ireland to a period subsequent to the twelfth century. His words, as given in "Good News from Ireland"[†] are—"Before the twelfth century Ireland had been celebrated for holiness and learning; but after the twelfth century, instead of scriptural schools, which had formerly abounded in Ireland, we see a large number of monastic houses built with the spoils of violence," etc. Dr. Reeves gives a very different account—"These sixth-century monasteries,"[‡] he says, " were as rapid in their growth as they were numerous in their creation. St. Finian's, of Clonard; St. Comgall's, of Bangor; and St. Brendan's, of Clonfert, each numbered 3,000 inmates." The same in-

---

[*] Church of St. Patrick, p. 85. [†] p. 158.
[‡] Vita Columbæ, p. 336.

formation is conveyed in every primer of Irish Church history.

St. Bernard, in his life of St. Malachy,[*] tells us that one Irish monk, St. Luan, who had been brought up at the convent of Bangor, founded one hundred monasteries.[†]

APPLICATION OF THE CANON OF ST. PATRICK.

Such an important canon as that of St. Patrick, having been passed in the very beginning of our history as a Christian nation, the next question which presents itself is—Do we find any instance where this canon was referred to or acted upon? Not at all, says Wilde, who quotes from King's history, as follows:—" At all events it appears certain that for 700 years after St. Patrick's arrival in Ireland in 432, no pope . . . . . ever heard any cause connected with this country, ... or was allowed in any other way to interfere with the concerns of the Church of this island until 1132"[‡]—and a little further on,[§] he continues "the first Abbot of Mellifont was Christian O'Conarchy, who, in 1145 was made Bishop of Lismore. He it was, who after-

---

[*] Vita St. Malachiæ, quoted by Montalembert in his Monks of the West, vol. ii. p. 396.

[†] See Haverty's History of Ireland, p. 91.

[‡] Boyne and Blackwater, p. 282.   [§] Ibid. p. 285.

wards presided at the Council of Cashel, held by order of Henry II. It was then and there the Irish Church became really dependent on that of England, and consequently of Rome, so that we may fairly trace the act to the influence of the first Abbot of Mellifont." It is pleasant in pursuing an historical inquiry, to find vague statements give place to definite references to time and place, as it enables one more easily to close with an adversary. The allegation adopted by Wilde, has at all events the merit of being above board, namely, for 700 years after the time of St. Patrick, no pope ever was allowed to interfere with the concerns of the Irish Church. Is this true? The answer to the question leads us at once to the Paschal controversy, which disturbed for a long time the peace of the Irish Church.

We have already seen that the Irish Church was founded by Pope Celestine, and that both Palladius and St. Patrick were sent from Rome to preach the Gospel in this country. How then did it occur that there should be any difference between the Irish and the Roman Church in the computation of the Easter time? Originally there was not any difference.* This is admitted by Rev. R. King,† who says—" The

---

* Lanigan, vol. ii. p. 379-384.
† Church Hist. vol. i. p. 143.

Churches of Britain, with whom the Irish were nearly or entirely agreed in this particular, used in the earliest times of which we have authentic accounts, to celebrate their Easter according to the system adopted by the Romans and other Christians of the west of Europe. This is distinctly stated by the Roman emperor Constantine the Great, in a letter addressed by him to the churches in his dominions, after the sitting of the famous Council of Nice, in which he says, that before that time (A.D. 325) one and the same Easter used to be " observed by all the Churches of the western, and southern, and northern parts of the world, and by some of those in eastern countries;" and in particular that this Easter was used " in the city of Rome, and all through Italy, in the provinces of Gaul, the BRITISH TERRITORIES," &c., &c.* King goes on to say—" In the course of time, however, the Romans found occasion to alter and correct the method used by them for calculating the time of their great festival; and these alterations were not adopted by the Britons and Irish, nor perhaps well understood by them in general, for a long time, owing, partly, it may be, to that interruption of communication between Rome and the British Isles, which was caused by the

* In vita Constantini, lib. iii. cap. 19.

Saxon troubles, and continued for a period of nearly 150 years, from the commencement of their invasions in A.D. 449, to the arrival of the Roman missionary Augustine in 596. Such appears to have been the origin of the differences concerning Easter between the Church of Rome, and the ancient British churches." This admission of King's is placed beyond dispute, by a work recently published in Rome. We learn from Count de Rossi's valuable volume on Roman Inscriptions,* that at the time of the Council of Arles, the cycle of 84 years for computing Easter was adopted throughout the entire Church, as appears from a letter sent by that council to Pope Sylvester, A.D. 314, in which these words are found—"Primo loco de observatione paschæ dominici, ut uno die et uno tempore per omnem orbem a nobis observetur et juxta consuetudinem, literas ad omnes tu dirigas." Van der Hagen has proved beyond all question, that the Roman Church, at the time of the Council of Arles, made use of the cycle of 84 years to fix the Paschal time. This same cycle of 84 years, observed in Rome and throughout the Christian world in the time of Pope Sylvester, was that which the Irish Church was called upon to abandon in the sixth century, and with which it

* Inscriptiones Christianæ urbis Romæ etc. Prolegomena, p. lxxxv.

showed such reluctance to part. There were British bishops present at the Council of Arles, " hence," observes De Rossi, " it requires very little sagacity to perceive that these bishops derived their cycle, and the manner of computing Easter, from Sylvester the Roman Pontiff, and the corrections and changes which were subsequently made did not reach them, as they were so much separated from the continent of Europe, as to be considered at the ends of the earth. Hence," continues the author, " we understand the origin of the celebrated controversies about the mode of celebrating Easter in the British Churches; thus the fable of the Eastern origin of the British Churches, and of their peculiar rite of Paschal time is exploded, and the union of the ancient British Churches with that of Rome is established by a new argument."

From these extracts it appears that originally there was no difference between the Irish or British Churches and the Roman Church on the subject of computing the Easter. Changes and corrections were, however, subsequently made in Rome, which, owing to the distance of Ireland from Rome, and to a variety of other circumstances remained quite unknown in Ireland as in England. In course of time the Irish were urged to conform to the general practice of the Church, which had received the corrections made in the calendar at Rome. An admonitory letter was received from Pope Honorius I., in 629, according to Ussher's Computation; others say in 634. In that letter, the pope called upon the Irish to give up the cycle of calculating Easter, which they had followed from the time of St. Patrick, and to receive the corrected calendar. Ven. Bede supplies us with an account of this very important proceeding. "The same Pope Honorius* sent letters to the Irish people, whom he found to err in the computation of Easter, in which he exhorted them not to esteem their own scanty little number, inhabiting the very ends of the earth, as wiser than the Churches of Christ, ancient and modern, throughout the world; and not to persevere in celebrating a different Easter from their's, in opposition to the Paschal computations and synodal decrees of the bishops of the whole world."

As this Paschal controversy lasted a long time, created considerable emotion in the Church of Ireland, and is referred to by Protestants to show that the Irish clergy, in this very question, refused to abide by the decision, or to acknowledge the supremacy of the Holy See, it cannot but be interesting to observe how the question was handled in the com-

* Bede, Hist. Eccl. lib. ii. c. 19.

mencement of the agitation. If the Protestant view
were correct, we should easily guess what course
would be adopted, by the heads of the Irish Church,
on receiving Pope Honorius' letter. They would at
once protest against any admonitory letter being
addressed to them by an authority which they denied,
and having forwarded a spirited rejection of assumed
jurisdiction, they would vindicate their own independence, by persisting resolutely in their celebration
of the Paschal time. Was this what occurred? By
no means.

THE SYNOD OF OLD LEIGHLIN.

In consequence of the pope's letter, a Synod was
at once convened at Old Leighlin, the history of
which is handed down by a learned monk named
Cummian, who belonged to the monastery founded
at Durrow by St. Columbkille.* His account of the
proceedings is this—" It was decreed by our seniors,
according to the command, that if any difference arise
between cause and cause, and opinions vary between
leprosy and no leprosy, they should go to the place
which the Lord had chosen; and if the cause was one
of the ' causæ majores,' *that it should be referred to*

* Lanigan, vol. i. p. 58 ; vol. ii. p. 398. St. Cummian died in
661 or 662. We have already referred to him at p. 69.

the Head of Cities, according to the synodical canon."*
Here, then, we find the command or decree to refer
difficulties to Rome for adjudication solemnly drawn
up and signed by St. Patrick and his associates assembled in synod; and two centuries later, when difficulties did arise, not even in matters of faith, but merely
of discipline, this decree of St. Patrick is assigned as
the reason why an appeal should be made to the Apostolic Seat, that is, the Chair of Peter.   Accordingly,
a deputation was sent to Rome, as we are thus
informed by Cummian, who was present at the
synod—"Misimus quos novimus sapientes et humiles
esse velut natos ad matrem."   "We sent those whom
we knew to be wise and humble, as children to their
mother."   Can any language be stronger to express
the respect, veneration, and loving obedience of the
Irish Church to that of Rome, from which she
sprung?   The result of the appeal was that on the
return of the deputation in three years, the new
Roman cycle and rules were universally adopted
throughout Leinster, Munster, and nearly all Connaught.   It is quite true that many of the Irish
showed a great unwillingness to give in, for a considerable time.   The question was not at all one
concerning a point of faith.   There was merely a

* Lanigan, vol. ii. c. 15, p. 391, and Rock, p. 60, etc.

difference in the manner of computing the time at which Easter should be celebrated; and the Irish, with that love of old usages for which the nation has at all times been remarkable, wished to preserve the system brought into this country as it had been by St. Patrick from Rome,* but subsequently altered there at the correction of the calendar. Many of the Irish thought that this diversity in a matter of discipline should be allowed the Irish Church through reverence for St. Patrick, St. Columbkille, and the other fathers of our national Church. The words of Cummian, in which he assigns his reasons for adopting the Roman cycle, and laying aside that which had been observed in Ireland, are remarkable. He was a monk of St. Columbkille's order, and addressed a most learned letter on this Paschal controversy to Segienus, Abbot of Iona, the head-quarters of the Columbian monks, who very reluctantly abandoned the practice of their founder. Cummian, in leading the way, and appealing to them to follow, quotes a passage from St. Jerome—" Ancient authority rises up against me; I, in the meanwhile, cry out—if any be joined to the Chair of St. Peter, that man is mine." " Antiqua in me insurgit auctoritas. Ego, interim clamito; si quis cathedræ sancti Petri jungatur meus

* Lanigan, vol. ii. p. 379.

est ille."* This was a most apposite citation—" The authority of Patrick, Columbkille, and others is against me, but I cannot separate myself from the Chair of St. Peter."

Goldwin Smith, in his able Essay on Irish History and Irish Character,† states, rather fairly, the nature of these differences regarding the time for celebrating Easter, which prevailed during part of the seventh century—" The division which undoubtedly existed between the Keltic Church in Ireland, Wales, and Scotland on the one hand, and the Churches which were under the complete dominion of Rome, on the other, was not so much a division of doctrine, as of ecclesiastical jurisdiction." There was no question of doctrine at all, but one merely of discipline.

St. Columbanus boldly stood up for the continuance of the Irish practice, and wrote letters to Popes Boniface IV. and Gregory the Great, to vindicate the traditional observance of Easter in the Irish Church.

These letters are appealed to by our adversaries, to show that the writer did not recognize the authority of the See of Rome. Yet these same letters contain

* See Todd's Church of St. Patrick, p. 111.
† Irish History and Irish Character, p. 29.

H

a distinct profession of that supremacy. The epistle to Pope Boniface commences thus, in the Rev. R. King's rendering:—*

" To the most honoured head of all the Churches of all Europe, that eminently exalted prelate, that pastor of pastors," etc., etc. Is that the language of Mr. Whiteside's co-religionists? If Pope Boniface were the head of all the Churches of all Europe, therefore was he the head of the Irish Church, according to our notions of logic.

Again Columbanus goes on†—" For it is as your friend, your disciple, not as an alien, that I shall speak, and therefore shall I use freedom in my words, as addressing myself to our master, and to those that are the governors and mystic helmsmen of the spiritual ship."

As St. Columbanus was so outspoken in this very letter, and maintained so boldly the practice of celebrating the Pasch followed in Ireland, and yet so fully acknowledges the dependence of the Irish Church on Rome, in the words just now quoted, belief in the supremacy of the Holy See must have been a very clearly-defined dogma of the Irish Church. Had there been any obscurity on this point,

* King's Church Hist. vol. iii. p. 940.
† Ibid. p. 942.

Columbanus was too able and too earnest not to assail
what clashed so severely with his cherished opinions on
the Paschal controversy. Hence the great importance
of those words, in which he sets forth the prerogatives
of the Holy See—"There has been among us no Jew,
nor heretic, nor schismatic, but the Catholic faith, as
it was delivered at the first by you, that is to say by
the successors of the holy apostles, is still maintained
among us with unshaken fidelity."[*] He goes on, "For
I promised to that party on your behalf that the
Church of Rome would never defend a heretic in opposition to the Catholic faith, a sentiment which it is but
proper for disciples to entertain concerning their
master. In order, then, that you may not lack apostolic honor, preserve the apostolic faith, confirm it by
your testimony, support it with your pen, fortify it
by the decision of a synod, so that none may be able
on rightful grounds to resist your authority. Slight
not this little word of advice offered by a stranger,
from any feeling connected with your consciousness
of being the teacher of him who is thus anxious on
your behalf." A little further on he says: "Therefore it is I have been led to cry, Awake to vigilance,
good Pope! for on you devolves the responsibility
of the danger which now threatens the whole army

[*] King's Church Hist. vol. iii. p. 942-944.

of the Lord, lying torpid as it is in the field. Every
thing is waiting for the signal from you, who are possessed of the legitimate power of regulating all details,
arranging the war, arousing the leaders, ordering to
arms, marshalling the lines, in fine, opening the
combat, yourself marching in the van.   For we
indeed, as I have already stated, are warmly attached
to the Chair of St. Peter; and great as is the re-
nown and celebrity of Rome, it is by means of that
chair alone that she is great and illustrious with us.
You are in a manner heavenly, if the expression may
be allowed, and Rome is the head of the Churches
of the world, saving the singular prerogative of the
place of the Lord's resurrection."*   How far the
last clause may affect the universal supremacy of the
Holy See, this is not the place to discuss; our object
is to show the dependence and submission of the Irish
Church upon Rome.   From these passages of this
celebrated letter then, it appears, according to Columbanus, that the pope whom he addressed was " the
most honoured head of all the Churches of Europe,
the pastor of pastors, the mystic helmsman of the
spiritual ship, the commander-in-chief of the entire

* St. Columbanus alluded to the *reverence* due to Jerusalem,
which, as is well known, claimed no *jurisdiction whatever* till it was
erected into a patriarchate in the fourth century.

army of the Lord, who was to give the signal and to regulate all the details." It is impossible to imagine language which would convey more forcibly the doctrine of the Papal supremacy. Let us suppose for a moment that the Protestant theory of the independence of the Irish Church was correct—what becomes of the language of Columbanus? Would not every line of it be falsified in such a supposition?—You are the head of all the churches, but not of ours. You are the pastor of pastors, but not of Irish pastors. You are the helmsman of the ship, but not our helmsman. You are the comman-der-in-chief, having the legitimate authority to regulate all the details, but not to regulate the *Irish Brigade*. You are almost heavenly, because seated in that Chair of St. Peter, which is great and illus-trious with us—that is, great and illustrious every-where else except with us—and Rome is the head of all the churches in the world, but Ireland is not in the world, but in the moon! Does not the Protes-tant theory make a complete burlesque of the power-ful and eloquent letter—whilst on the other hand, every expression falls in perfectly with the doctrine of the Papal supremacy over the Church of old Ireland?

Notwithstanding the clear expressions of Colum-banus upon the supremacy of the pope, it is at the same time undeniable that he was far from being an upholder of the infallibility of the pope. He manifestly held upon this point the same opinions as were supported in the seventeenth century by Bossuet and the other leaders of the Gallican party. In his letter to Boniface IV., he says[*]—"Lest, therefore, the old enemy should succeed in entangling mankind in this interminable cord of error, let the occasion of the schism, I implore of you, be cut off at once, with the knife, as we may say, of St. Peter, that is, by (setting forth) a true confession of the faith in a synod, and expressions of abomination and anathema against all heretics, that (so) you may purge the Chair of Peter from all error, if there have been any, as they say, introduced; if not, that its purity may be acknowledged on all hands; for it is a painful and lamentable case if the Catholic faith be not held in the Apostolic See." Upon these expressions Dr. Todd remarks[†]—" If the language of St. Columbanus, in the passages already quoted, be opposed to the modern teaching of Rome, there are yet other places in this letter still more irreconcilable with the high views of Papal supremacy that have gained currency since his time." This is very illogical

[*] King's Hist. vol. iii. p. 949.
[†] Church of St. Patrick, p. 130.

upon the part of Dr. Todd. Queen Victoria is the supreme ruler of Great Britain, and supreme head of the English Established Church, yet that does not involve her infallibility. Columbanus openly maintained the supremacy of the pope, and as openly denied his infallibility, when not taken in conjunction with the voice of a general council. But that infallibility is not and never has been a point of Catholic faith; and unless Dr. Todd would make out the illustrious Bossuet to have been no Catholic, then he cannot lay any claim upon Columbanus; for their views were precisely similar. Now-a-days there are very few supporters of such opinions as were upheld by the Gallican school; they are almost universally regarded as unsound and extreme; yet they are not opposed to any defined doctrine of Catholicity, but merely to the general sense of the Church, which rejects them as untrue.

In another letter to the same Pope Boniface—Columbanus, writing in support of the Irish practice of celebrating Easter, says—" With the due performance of our homage, we pour out our prayers only to thee, through our Lord Jesus Christ and the Holy Ghost, and through the unity of faith which is common to us, that thou wouldst bestow upon us, labouring pilgrims, the solace of thy holy sentence, with which

thou mayest strengthen the tradition of our elders,
if it is not against faith; with which we may be
enabled, through thy adjudication, to keep the rite of
Easter as we got it from our forefathers."* " Cum salu-
tationum condignis officiis preces tantum ad te (Boni-
facium Papam) per Dom. nostrum Jesum Christum et
Spiritum Sanctum, et per unitatem fidei nostræ quæ
invicem est, fundimus, ut nobis peregrinis laboranti-
bus tuæ piæ sententiæ præstes solatium, quo si non
contra fidem est, nostrorum traditionem robores senio-
rum, quo ritum Paschæ sicut accepimus a majoribus,
observare per tuum possimus judicium in nostra pere-
grinatione." Comment upon this is quite superfluous.

Again the saint says—" We ask for peace and
ecclesiastical unity, such as that which St. Polycarp
maintained with Pope Anicetus, and for permission
to observe 'our own laws, according to the regulation made by the hundred and fifty Fathers of the
Council of Constantinople."†

A few years pass over, and the Irish practices have
given way to those of Rome.

" This final submission," observes an author from
whose treatise we have borrowed much,‡ " is a con-

* Quoted by Rock, p. 44.
† See Dublin Review, June, 1846, p. 494.
‡ Most Rev. Dr. Cullen's Essay, p. 17.

vincing proof of their acknowledgment of dependence upon Rome. Neither the warmth of controversy, nor hatred to what they considered an innovation, nor their excessive attachment to the usages approved of and practised by St. Columbkille, were of avail in opposition to the authority of the Holy See."

THE INDIRECT PROOFS OF THE PAPAL SUPREMACY.

We have hitherto treated of the direct proofs of the dependence of the Irish Church upon that of Rome, namely, the decrees of synods, the appeals to Rome, the judgment pronounced at Rome, and obeyed in Ireland. We come now to consider the collateral evidence in support of the same point It is admitted on all hands that the Christian Churches of France, England, Germany, Belgium, Switzerland, and Italy were at this period in strict communion with the Holy See, and that this connexion was founded on the belief of the Supremacy of that See; such supremacy was a dogma received in these Churches. If the Irish Church rejected that dogma, then would those Churches be separated from her by a clear boundary-line of faith—and the Irish would be regarded as cut off by heresy from the communion of the other Churches of Europe. Did any such

estrangement exist? Was any difference of belief
manifested in the relations of the Ancient Irish
Church with those of the rest of Europe? Not the
least—but on the contrary the closest interchange,
social, educational, and religious, existed during all
the period of Ireland's glorious career, from the
coming of St. Patrick in the fifth century to the
invasions of the Danes, three hundred years later.
Columbanus founded successively three monasteries
in France—at Luxeuil, and in the neighbourhood.
To these monasteries the French youth crowded in hundreds to drink in learning and religion. Would such
have been the case, were there not identity of belief
between the Irish and French Church? The single
Monastery of Luxeuil, in the short period of twenty
years, supplied five bishops to the sees of France.[*]
Would these monks, who, according to our opponents,
rejected the authority of the Holy See, have been
placed as spiritual rulers over a people who held a
different faith on this leading and prominent characteristic of the Catholic Church? It is impossible for
one moment to admit such a glaring absurdity.

St. Columbanus, owing to the intrigues of a profli-
gate king and his abandoned mother, whose immo-
rality and wickedness the intrepid monk rebuked,

* King's Church Hist. vol. i. p. 277.

was obliged to leave France. He proceeded along
the banks of the Rhine to Switzerland, and having
laboured there for some time in the conversion of
souls, left after him one of his companions, St. Gall,
an Irishman, who founded a celebrated monastery,
which gave its name, still retained, to the town and
canton in which the monastery flourished. Columbanus then crossed the Alps into Italy, and there in
a gorge of the Appenines, not far from Milan, established his Monastery of Bobbio, which became so famous
in after times. It possessed the best library in Europe
during the middle ages, and continued its useful
career for eleven hundred years, till suppressed in
the violent efforts made at the close of the last century by the French Revolution to root out all religion
from the world. A remarkable proof of the acknowledgment of the Pope's supremacy is supplied by an
incident which occured in connexion with this
Monastery of Bobbio. St. Columbanus, the founder,
did not place his monasteries under episcopal control.
Bertolf was the second Abbot of Bobbio after Columbanus. In his time an attempt was made to reduce
the monastery under the rule of a neighbouring
bishop. Bertolf resisted; made a journey to Rome
to obtain the protection of Pope Honorius I., and
obtained a privilege from the Apostolic See, pro-

hibiting any bishop from attempting to exercise jurisdiction in the aforesaid community upon any plea whatsoever.* Now if the teachings of Columbanus instructed his followers to reject the authority of the Holy See, would such an appeal be made by his immediate successors, and if made, would it be listened to? Would not the Pope at once reply— " You separate yourselves from the rest of Christian Europe. You set up for an independence of your own, and reject the belief of the whole Church. Why seek my protection whilst you refuse to admit my authority and jurisdiction? Go to your own superiors with your appeal." But on the other hand, being in the words of Columbanus himself, " the commander-in-chief, having the legitimate authority to settle all the details," he at once extended to this Irish foundation the assistance which it sought, and confirmed its privilege of freedom from episcopal jurisdiction.

St. Columbanus, whose foundations on the continent we have slightly glanced at, was educated in the Monastery of Bangor, near Belfast. The spectacle which Ireland then presented is one of which every Irishman should feel justly proud. Placed at the extreme west of Europe—separated by seas from

* King's Church History, vol. i. p. 275.

the continent, and thus spared the devastations of Hun, Goth, and Vandal, which overthrew the Roman Empire, and laid waste its fair provinces, Ireland devoted herself heart and soul to the great work of propagating the true religion. She grounded those who flocked to her schools in the fear of the Lord, and civilized and elevated their minds by the cultivation of literature. Montalembert thus eloquently depicts this period of Irish history*—" From the moment that this green Erin, situated at the extremity of the known world, had seen the sun of faith rise upon her, she had vowed herself to it with an ardent and tender devotion, which became her very life. The course of ages has not interrupted this; the most bloody and implacable of persecutions has not shaken it; the defection of all northern Europe has not led her astray; and she maintains still amid the splendour and miseries of modern civilization and Anglo-Saxon supremacy, an inexhaustible centre of faith, where survives along with the completest orthodoxy, that admirable purity of manners which no conqueror and no adversary has ever been able to dispute, to equal, or diminish. The ecclesiastical antiquity and hagiography of Ireland constitute an entire world of inquiry. The productiveness of the

* Monks of the West, vol. ii. p. 389, 396-7, etc.

monastic germ planted by Patrick and Bridget was prodigious; for shortly the monasteries of Bangor, Clonfert, and elsewhere became entire towns, each of which enclosed more than three thousand cenobites. There was besides an intellectual development which the eremites of Egypt had not known. The Irish communities joined by the monks from Gaul and Rome, whom the example of Patrick had drawn upon his steps, entered into rivalry with the great monastic schools of Gaul. They explained Ovid there; they copied Virgil; they devoted themselves especially to Greek literature; they drew back from no inquiry—from no discussion ; they gloried in placing boldness upon a level with faith.*   A

---

* The wondrous excellence attained by the Irish in the art of illuminating has never been equalled. The Book of Kells, preserved in Trinity College, is unrivalled in the beauty of design and intricacy of execution which it displays. Digby Wyatt, in his valuable work on the Art of Illuminating, bears the amplest testimony to the excellencies of the Irish school—"At a period, as Mr. Westwood declares, when the arts may be said to have been almost extinct in Italy and other parts of the continent—namely, from the fifth to the end of the eighth century—a style of art had been established and cultivated in Ireland, absolutely distinct from that of all other parts of the civilised world. There is abundant evidence to prove that in the sixth and seventh centuries, the art of ornamenting manuscripts of the Sacred Scriptures, and especially of the Gospels, had attained a perfection in Ireland almost marvellous. In delicacy of handling, and minute but faultless execution, the whole range of palæography offers nothing comparable to these early Irish manuscripts, and those produced

characteristic still more distinctive of the Irish monks, as of all their nation, was the imperious necessity of spreading themselves without, of seeking or carrying knowledge and faith afar, and of penetrating into the most distant regions to watch or combat paganism; this monastic nation, therefore, became the missionary nation par excellence. While some came to Ireland to procure religious instruction, the Irish missionaries launched forth from their island; they covered the

in the same style in England. When in Dublin some years ago, I had the opportunity of studying very carefully the most marvellous of all, the Book of Kells, some of the ornaments of which I attempted to copy, but broke down in despair. Of this very book Mr. Westwood examined the pages, as I did, for hours together without ever detecting a false line or an irregular interlacement. In one space of about a quarter of an inch superficial, he counted with a magnifying glass no less than 158 interlacements of a slender ribbon pattern, formed of white lines edged by black ones upon a black ground. No wonder that tradition should allege that these unerring lines should have been traced by angels." Westwood informs us in his Palæographia Sacra that "the chief peculiarities of the Irish school consist in the illumination of the first page of each of the sacred books, the letters of the first few words, and more especially the initial, being represented of a very large size, and highly ornamented in patterns of the most intricate design, with marginal rows of red dots, the classical acanthus being never represented." Again he says of the Irish MSS.— "The series of MSS. from which the facsimiles in the accompanying plate we have copied (in conjunction with the Book of Kells), constitute a series of actual proofs still preserved in Ireland of the existence of a religious and national school of art in that country at a period when the rest of Europe was almost involved in mental darkness."

land and seas of the west. Unwearied navigators,
they landed on the most desert islands; they overflowed the continent with their successive emigrations;
they saw in incessant visions a world known and unknown to be conquered for Christ."

As the Irish missionaries overflowed other countries,
so did the Irish schools attract countless multitudes
of strangers in pursuit of learning to our shores.
" Then sprung up* the celebrated schools of Armagh,
Bangor, Lismore, Durrow, Clonard, etc., which were
frequented by numberless disciples, not only from
Ireland, but from England and the different countries
of Europe." St. Bernard, in his Life of St. Malachy,
says of Bangor,† that it was a very holy place,
and the fruitful mother of saints—that monks reared
within its enclosures not only filled Ireland and Scotland, but that they spread themselves in great numbers throughout other countries. And Alcuin, in a
letter to the brethren in Ireland, declares that " he is
very much rejoiced to find that our Lord Jesus still
had, in the renowned island of Erin, so many wor-

---

* La Chiesa d'Irlanda, p. 18, Essay by Most Rev. Dr. Cullen.
† "Locus vere sanctus, fecundus que sanctorum. Hiberniam,
Scotiam que repleverunt genimina ejus. Nec modo in præfatas
sed in exteras etiam regiones, quasi inundatione facta, illa se
sanctorum examina effuderunt."—Vitæ Malachiæ.

·shippers of his holy name, so many preachers of the true faith, and so many followers of heavenly wisdom, as had been reported to him. In former ages the most learned masters were wont to issue forth from Ireland, and to pass into Britain, Gaul, and Italy."

In the schools of Ireland were kindled that zeal and devotion which gave so many apostles to the Churches of Europe. If these men taught sound doctrine on the supremacy of the Holy See,—if the Churches founded by them were subject to the jurisdiction of the Popes, it is manifest that they must have learned that doctrine in the famous schools of Ireland, where they had been educated. The history of the "ages of faith" records, that the Irish missionaries founded monasteries, and governed churches in France, Germany, Belgium, Switzerland, and Italy, and thus formed the closest alliance in religion with those countries which confessedly acknowledged the supremacy of the Holy See. How then can it be pretended that their faith was different from the belief of the countries with which they were so completely identified?

Dr. Lynch, in his work entitled Cambrensis Eversus, details at considerable length the migrations of the Irish monks. As the labours of our early missionaries are too little known and appreciated, we subjoin a valuable extract bearing on this subject:—[*]

"All the world knows that the Irish went over, not one by one, but in crowds, to Britain, Gaul, Belgium, and Germany, to convert the inhabitants of those regions to the Christian religion, and bring them under the obedience of the Roman Pontiff. A signal testimony to this fact is found in the letter of Eric of Auxerre to Charles the Bald: 'Need I mention Ireland, who, despising the dangers of the deep, emigrates to our shores, with almost the entire host of her philosophers; the most eminent amongst them become voluntary exiles, to minister to the wishes of our most wise Solomon.' Such, also, is the testimony of St. Bernard: 'From Ireland, as from an overflowing stream, crowds of holy men descended on foreign nations.' Walefridus Strabo says, 'that the habit of emigrating had become a second nature to the Scoti,' namely, the Irish, as I have already proved; hence the just observation of Osborne, that the habit of emigrating had taken the strongest hold of the Irish; for what the piety of other nations has made a habit, they have changed from habit into nature. Those holy emigrations of the Irish were distinguished by

---

[*] Cambrensis Eversus, vol. ii. c. 25.

a peculiarity never, or but very seldom, found among
other nations. As soon as it became known that any
eminent monk had resolved to undertake one of these
sacred expeditions, twelve men of the same order
placed themselves under his command, and were
selected to accompany him; a custom probably introduced by St. Patrick, who had been ably supported
by twelve chosen associates, in converting the Irish
from the darkness of paganism to the light of the
true faith. St. Rioch, nephew to St. Patrick, and
walking in his footsteps, was attended, in his sacred
missions to foreign tribes and regions, by twelve col-
leagues of his own order; and when St. Rupert, who
had been baptized by a nephew of St. Patrick, apostle
of Ireland, departed to draw down the fertilizing
dews of true religion on pagan Bavaria, twelve faithful companions shared the perils and labours of his
journey and mission. St. Finnian, bishop of Clonard,
selected twelve from the thronged college of his disciples, to devote them in a special manner to establish
and animate the principles of the Christian religion
among the Irish, and hence they were styled by pos-
terity the twelve apostles of Ireland. St. Columba
was accompanied in his apostolic mission to Albany
by twelve monks. Twelve followed St. Finbar in
his pilgrimage beyond the seas, and twelve St. Mai-

doc, bishop of Ferns, in one of his foreign missions.
St. Colman Fin was never seen without his college
of twelve disciples. When the ceaseless eruptions of
foreign enemies, or the negligence of the bishops,
had well nigh extinguished the virtue of religion in
Gaul, and left nothing but the Christian Faith—
when the medicine of penance and love of mortification were found nowhere, or but with a few, 'then,'
says Jonas, 'St. Columbanus descended on Gaul,
supported by twelve associates, to arouse her from
her torpor, and enlighten her sons with the beams of
the most exalted piety.' Twelve disciples followed
St. Eloquius from Ireland to illumine the Belgians
with the rays of faith; twelve accompanied St.
Willibrod from Ireland to Germany; the pilgrimage and labours of St. Farrannan in Belgium were
shared by twelve faithful brothers of the cowl; and
the same number were fellow-exiles with St. Ma-
callan. Perhaps the reason why the Irish clung
with such invincible attachment to this custom, was
the number of the apostles chosen by our Saviour,
and the same number of disciples appointed by the
Apostolic See to accompany Palladius to Ireland.

" But it was not in companies of twelve alone that
great men went forth from Ireland to plant or re-
vive sound doctrine and discipline in foreign lands.

Bodies far more numerous are also mentioned. St. Albert was accompanied by nineteen disciples; sixty accompanied St. Brendan in his voyage in search of the land of promise; St. Guigner, son of the king of Ireland, passed over to Britain with a noble band of seven hundred and seventy associates; and St. Blaithmac, son of the king of Ireland, was followed thither by a good number of monks. St. Donnanus led away from his country fifty-two associates. Twenty-four disciples of St. Ailbe were sent by him to propagate the faith in Iceland. St. Emilius brought to the aid of St. Fursa, at Lagny, a large body of their countrymen, and gave him wonderful aid in instilling the grace of God into the souls of man. St. Seizen was accompanied by seventy disciples to Armoric Britain; and Alsace welcomed St. Florentius with Argobastus and Hidulph. Irish saints are also found toiling in strange lands, in smaller numbers, and fortifying them abundantly with the dew of their faith and virtues. In Italy there were Donatus of Fiesule, Andrew, and their sister St. Brigid of Opaca; in Picardy, SS. Caidoc and Fricorius, otherwise Adrian; at Rheims, SS. Gibrian, Tressan, Hœlan, Abram, German, Veran, Petroan, Promptia, Possenna, and Iruda; at Paris, Claude, Clement, and John; among the Morini (of

Boulogne), SS. Vulgan, Kilian, and Obod; in the territory of Beauvais, SS. Maura and Brigid, virgins and martyrs, and their brother Hyspad; at Fusciria, SS. Marildis, virgin, and her brother Alexander. In Kleggon, a district in Germany, St. Northberga, with Sista, and nine others of her children. At Ra-. tisbon, SS. Marian, John, Candidus, Clement, Murcherdach, Magnoald, and Isaac. In Austrasia, SS. Kilian, Colonatus, and Totnan; and St. Cadroe and his associates at Walcedore. These devoted their lives to the instruction of the people, and were celebrated for the miraculous favours obtained by their intercession.

" Though it would be too tedious to mention in detail the great number of our countrymen who were distinguished on the Continent for their marvellous works and the sanctity of their lives, it would be unpardonable to omit them altogether. Not taking into account those who were canonized in Britain, nor those who went over to the continent in large bodies, we have in Italy, St. Cathaldus, patron of Tarentum, St. Donatus, patron of Fiesole, St. Emilian, patron of Faventum, and St. Frigidian of Lucca. Pavia honors John Albinus as the founder of her university, and St. Cumean is, above all other Irish saints, the favorite patron of Bobbio.

"In Gaul, St. Mansuetus is patron of Tulle, St. Finlag, abbot of St. Simphonan, patron of Metz, and St. Præcordius, of Corbie, situated between Amiens and Peronne. Amiens honors St. Forcensius, and Poitiers, St. Fridolinus, abbot of the monastery of St. Hilary. St. Elias is patron of Angouleme, St. Anatolius of Besançon, St. Fiacre of Meaux, St. Fursa of Peronne, and St. Laurence of Eu. Liege honors St. Momo, and Strasburg SS. Florentius and Arbogastus. In Bretagne, SS. Origin, Toava, Tenan, Gildas, Brioc, and many others, are revered as patrons. In Rheims and the surrounding district, SS. Gibrian, Heran, German, Veran, Abran, Petrans and three sisters, are held in the highest veneration. 'In Burgundy, the vineyard of the Lord yielded an abundant harvest to the zeal of St. Columbanus, who founded there a great number of monasteries and colleges of monks, restored the true service of God, and left there after him Deicolus, Columbinus, and Anatolius.' —Flodoard, *Hist. Rhemes.*

"In Burgundy, also, St. Maimbode is honored as a martyr.

"In Belgium, you have in Brabant, SS. Rumold, Fredegand, Himelin, Dympna, and Gerebernus. In Flanders, SS. Levin, Guthagon, Columbanus; in Artois, SS. Liugluio, Liuglianus, Kilian, Vulgan,

Fursa, and Obodius; in Hainault, SS. Ette, Adalgi-
sus, Abel, Wasnulph, and Mombolus; in Namur,
SS. Farennan, and Eloquius; in Liege, SS. Ultan,
Foillan, and Bertuin; in Gueldress, SS. Wiro, Ple-
chelm and Othger; in Holland, St. Hiero; in Fries-
land, SS. Suitbert and Acca.

"But Germany especially was the most flourishing
vineyard of our saints. St. Albuin, or Witta, is
honored as apostle in Thuringia; St. Disibode, at
Treves; St. Erhard, in Alsace and Bavaria; St. Fri-
dolin, in the Grisons of Switzerland; St. Gall among
the Suabians, Swiss, and Rhœtians; St. John in
Mecklenburg; St. Virgil, at Salzburg; St. Killian,
in Franconia; St. Rupert, in part of Bavaria. From
these saints these different places received the grace
of faith and the sacred discipline of Christian virtue,
and afterwards honored the memory of their bene-
factors as the apostles of their nation. But these are
not the only saints to whom the Germans send up
their filial prayers; equal honors are paid by them to
some others of our countrymen. St. Albert is honored at Ratisbon, SS. Deicola and Fintan at Con-
stance, and St. Eusebius in Coire. The town and
canton of St. Gall took their name from our countryman, St. Gall. 'This monastery,' says Munster, ' was
the school of the noble and the peasant, and the

nursery of a great number of learned men; at one period it contained no less than one hundred and fifty students and brothers.' Ireland was, therefore, both the athenæum of learning and the temple of holiness, supplying the world with literati and Heaven with saints. Truly doth she appear the academy of the Earth and the colony of Heaven. Was ever panegyric more appropriate than the words of Eric of Auxerre? 'Need I mention Ireland, who, despising the dangers of the deep, emigrates to our shores, with almost the whole host of her philosophers; the most eminent among them become voluntary exiles to minister to the tastes of our wisest Solomon?'"

We make no apology for the length of this extract. Many Irish Catholics travel every summer through France, Germany, Belgium, Switzerland, and Italy. In inspecting foreign churches, their interest is seldom awakened at viewing the mementoes in sculpture or painting of Irish saints, whose names are fondly cherished and deeply venerated abroad, but, unhappily, are unknown or forgotten at home.

CHAPTER V.

Section I.

CELIBACY OF THE CLERGY.

WE have seen, during the course of this inquiry, that the Ancient Church of Ireland was identical in teaching with the Catholic Church of to-day, in every point of faith that distinguishes Catholics from Protestants.   The Church of our fathers taught fourteen hundred years ago precisely what we believe on the Real Presence, the sacrifice of the Mass, prayers for the dead, and Masses for the repose of the soul, purgatory, the invocation of saints, special reverence and veneration for the Mother of God, miraculous interposition, obedience and submission to the "Apostolic Seat," and the necessity of fasting and mortification.   Mr. Whiteside, in a lecture lately delivered, upon the Life and Death of the Irish Parliament, undertook to inform us that the Irish Catholic clergy were permitted to marry. His words are:—" Lord Coke expressly states in

his chapter on Ireland, in the 4th institute, that at
a 'synod holden in Ireland by St. Patrick, their
apostle, it was unanimously agreed that Irish priests
should have wives.' Thus we are assured, by the
practice of the ancient Church in Ireland, that the
clergy were, and wisely, married men." Lord Coke
is here set forth as one of those "'soundest of antiquaries," who are the guiding light of Mr. Whiteside. It requires very little knowledge of history to
be aware that, great as was the authority of Lord
Coke on a point of English law, no one ever accused
him of knowing anything about Irish history. But
the lecturer can appeal to the testimony of a Catholic judge in support of his views. Justice Keogh,
in the case of Beamish *v.* Beamish, delivered the
following opinion on the 20th February, 1857:—

" It was not, as some vulgarly suppose, a fact that
priests in the Roman Catholic Church were never
allowed to marry—that celibacy was always enjoined
in the Church. It was a fact that, down to a late
period, priests and bishops in the Roman Catholic
Church were allowed to marry, and did marry. To
the year A.D. 1015 priests were allowed to marry,
and the vow of celibacy was not required until the
year 1076." What more can be required than this
impartial admission of one of the ablest judges on

the Irish bench to support the authority of the most eloquent orator at the Irish Bar?

We must submit to the imputation of being classed with "the vulgar" who dispute these statements of the learned judge. The Rev. R. King,* whose opinion we consider far more valuable on Irish history than that of either the English or Irish judge quoted against us, says—" The idea of the necessity or paramount importance of celibacy, as a rule for the clergy, prevailed at a very early period in most parts of the Church, and although 'from the beginning it was not so,' yet few instances of the contrary can be cited from our ancient writers; so that the general practice of our forefathers in this matter would appear to have been pretty much in accordance with the law which was afterwards introduced," and we may add utterly at variance with the statements of Judge Keogh, that celibacy was only introduced in the eleventh century. Again, in another place† Mr. King says—"We would guard our readers against errors, and not lead them to suppose that the Irish Christians of the seventh century agreed more nearly with ourselves than they really did, according to the accounts of them given

---

* Church Hist. vol. i. p. 370.   † Vol. i. p. 316.

in ancient histories. There are points connected
with Columbanus—such, for instance, as his views
concerning vows and monastic celibacy,—which mark
a clear distinction between his system and our own."
We entrust that extract to Judge Keogh's careful
consideration, when he next volunteers to place the
judicial stamp of " vulgarity" upon those who venture to differ from him as to the celibacy of the
early Irish clergy. Were we to grant the accuracy ·
of Mr. Whiteside's views upon this question, it would
only show that the early Irish Church, whilst identical with our Church of to-day in matters of faith,
differed from us in one respect in a mere question of
discipline. Taking that for granted, we are treated
to this beautiful specimen of logic :—" As the early
Irish Church differed in a point of discipline from
the Roman Catholic Church of to-day, with which
it was identical in faith, therefore it was the same
Church as the Protestant Church of to-day, from
which it differed in every point of doctrine !"

Instead of taking as our authorities an English
judge, who knew nothing about the history of Ireland, or an Irish barrister, whose lecture on the Irish
Parliament is filled with historical errors, let us consult the great saints of the Irish Church, who were
the brightest ornaments of " the Ages of Faith."

Amongst a host of the illustrious dead we select, St. Columbkille, or Columba, and St. Columbanus. As St. Columbkille flourished early in the sixth century, we may suppose him to be thoroughly in possession of the spirit and letter of St. Patrick's teaching. Dr. Reeves* says of St. Columbkille and his monks— "There can be no doubt that celibacy was strictly enjoined in his community, and the condition ' virgo corpore virgo mente' held up for imitation. Hence the total absence of anything like hereditary succession in the Abbacy of Hy." Again, the same authority tells us what were the characteristics of St. Columbkille's foundation†—" Few bishops and many priests, they celebrated different Masses, and followed different rules in the liturgy; they rejected the administration of women, and forbade them entrance to the monasteries." From this extract it appears that the " many priests" of the order were not allowed to marry, and that women were forbidden even to be servants throughout the numerous foundations of Columba.

The Rev. R. King gives a similar description of

---

* Notes on Adamnan's Work, p. 344.

† Pauci episcopi, et multi presbyteri, diversas Missas celebrabant et diversas regulas ; abnegabant mulierum administrationem, separantes eas a monasteriis.—Adamnan's Work, p. 334.

the monasteries established by St. Columbanus*—
" Within less, perhaps, than twenty years from the
death of Columbanus, Luxieu alone produced five
bishops, whose sees were situated in different parts
of France; and as for monasteries under his rule,
there was no end of them. . . . . And so much did
the mischievous rage for monastic celibacy come into
fashion generally at the time, that almost all France,
ere long, became studded over with convents, not
only for men, but for women also."

The Missal of Columbanus, already described as
found in the Monastery of Bobbio, and now preserved
in the Ambrosian Library at Milan, contains the following canon on this subject:—" If any cleric,
after entering holy orders, should again live with his
wife, he would be guilty of adultery."† Could this
be said if the priests were allowed to marry? Clearly
not; and even if married before priesthood, they
could no longer live with their wives.

There is extant a treatise by St. Columbanus, entitled " Liber de Penitentiarum Mensura Taxanda."
From it we learn that clergymen, when they had
taken holy orders, were bound to separate from the

---

* Church Hist. vol. i. p. 277.

† Si quis clericus vel superior gradus, qui uxorem habuit, et
post honorem iterum eam cognoverit, sciat se adulterium commis-
sisse.

wives they had married before ordination. The twentieth clause is as follows:—* "If any cleric or deacon, or in any orders, who had been a layman in the world with sons and daughters, after devoting himself to God, should again live with his wife, and beget a son of her, let him know that he has committed adultery, and has fallen into as great a sin as if from his youth he had been a cleric, and had communication with a girl to whom he was not married; because he offended *after his vow*, and after he consecrated himself to God, and he has made void his vow, therefore, he shall do penance for seven years on bread and water."

Dr. Lanigan justly remarks† that the rules of this Penitential were, in all probability, founded on the practices of the Irish Church; for Columbanus did not leave Ireland till he was upwards of fifty years of age, and had, of course, grown old in the ways of the Christian community with whom he had so long sojourned.

---

* "Si quis autem clericus, aut diaconus vel alicujus gradus, qui laicus fuit in seculo cum filiis et filiabus, post conversionem suam iterum suam cognoverit clientelam, et filium iterum de ea gennerit, sciat se adulterium perpetrasse, et non minus peccasse quam si ab juventute sua clericus fuisset et cum puella aliena peccasset, quia post votum suum peccavit, postquam se Domino consecravit et votum suum irritum fecit, idcirco similiter septem annis in pane et aqua peniteat."   † Eccl. Hist. vol. iv. p. 367.

The learned Abbot Cummian, who was a contemporary of St. Columbanus, has left us a "Penitential" which, happily, is preserved. It contains a canon condemning the marriage, not only of a monk, but likewise *of any cleric, after he had devoted himself to God,*—that is, after taking holy orders—and sentencing the delinquent to a penance of ten years, three of which he was to fast on bread and water, and to separate himself from the woman he had married. If he be unwilling to obey, let him be excommunicated by a synod, or by the Apostolic See.[*]

This canon of the seventh century is remarkable, not only as proving the obligation of celibacy on the part of monks, and of all other clerics, who had taken holy orders, but also as ordaining the appeal to the Apostolic See for the punishment of delinquents.

Another contemporary of Columbanus was St. Molua, who was educated under the care of the renowned Comgall of Bangor. He retired to Slieve

---

[*] "Si clericus aut monachus, postquam se Deo voverit, ad secularem habitum iterum reversus fuerit, aut uxorem duxerit, decem annis peniteat, tribus ex his in pane et aqua, et nunquam postea in conjugio copuletur. Quod si noluerit, sancta synodus vel *sedes apostolica* separavit eos a communione et convocationibus catholicorum."—Lanigan's Eccl. Hist. vol. iv. p. 367.

Bloom, and there established a monastery; he afterwards returned to Munster, of which province he
was a native, and founded several monastic houses.
He drew up a particular rule for his monks; one of
the regulations prescribed the perpetual exclusion of
women.*

In the venerable cathedral of Christ Church, Dublin, a synod was held towards the close of the twelfth
century (1186). Gerald Barry, an English priest,
who came over as a chaplain, in the train of the
conquerors, was present at that synod. In his
writings, he attacks the Irish nation in terms of the
fiercest invective, and was one of the most unscrupu-
lous slanderers that ever wrote against this country;
yet, in his general account of the Irish clergy, he
speaks most favourably of them. "The clergy of
this country are very commendable for religion, and
among divers virtues which distinguish them, *excel*
and are pre-eminent in the prerogative of chastity.†"

It is to be carefully observed that Gerald Barry
does not limit this prerogative of chastity to the

* " Ut nulla mulier ibi semper (*i.e.* in sempiternum) intraret, et
ab illo die usque hodie nulla mulier in illud monasterium audet
intrare."—Lanigan, vol. ii. p. 206.

† "Est autem terræ istius clerus satis religione commendabilis; et
inter varias quibus pollet virtutes, castitatis prerogativa præeminet
et præcellit."—Lanigan, vol. iv. p. 267.

monks, but extends it to all the clergy of the country. The canons agreed to in this synod are still extant, and are preserved among the archives of Christ Church. The thirteenth canon is as follows:— " Since the clergy of Ireland, among other virtues, have been always remarkably eminent for their chastity, and that it would be ignominious if they should be corrupted through his (the archbishop's) negligence, by the foul contagion of strangers, and the example of a few incontinent men, he therefore forbids, under the penalty of losing both office and benefice, that any priest, deacon, or subdeacon should keep any woman in their houses under the pretence of necessary service, or any other colour whatsoever, unless a mother, own sister, or such a person, whose age should remove all suspicion of any unlawful intercourse."*

It is manifest from the testimony of Gerald Barry, and the words of this canon, that celibacy was enjoined and observed by the Irish clergy, and that they had been always remarkably pre-eminent for chastity; whilst, for the preservation of that virtue, laws are enjoined to perpetuate the character which they had at all previous times deserved.

* Lanigan, vol. iv. p. 270.

Our views derive a strong confirmation from the ancient Catalogue of Irish Saints already quoted.*

This document of the seventh century describes three orders of Irish saints, commencing with St. Patrick, and extending over a period of more than two hundred years from his time. We are told that " the first order of Catholic saints was in the time of Patrick. They did not shun the services and society of women; because founded, as they were, on the rock Christ, they were not afraid of the blast of temptation. This order of saints lasted during four reigns," or in other words, for a space of one hundred years. The author's meaning is obvious; namely, that so exalted was the character of these founders of our Church, that no danger to their chastity, and no suspicion, could attach to them, in allowing the services of women, who attended to their necessary household wants. " The second order of Catholic presbyters; for in this order there were few bishops and many priests, to the number of three hundred. . . . They dispensed with the services of women, separating them from the monasteries. This order continued during four reigns more, ... and their names are these:—the two Finians, two Brendans, Jarlath of

* See p. 31.

Tuam, Comgall, Coemgen (St. Kevin), Ciaran, Columba, Cainech, etc., etc., and many others."

" The third order of saints was of this sort; they were holy priests, and few bishops, a hundred in number, who inhabited desert places, and lived on herbs and water and the alms of the faithful, and had no property of their own," etc.

The Rev. R. King, who gives the catalogue in full,* seeing that he cannot dispute the age or authenticity of this valuable document, and therefore cannot deny its account of celibacy as enjoined and practised in the earliest ages of our Christianity, endeavours to pass away with a sneer from the unwelcome insight into the discipline of our forefathers among the clergy—" Seclusion from the society of women," he observes, "living on herbs and alms, and retirement to a hermit's cave, are at least but dubious tests of real sanctity."

Having now passed briefly in review such numerous proofs of the discipline of the Irish Catholic Church, relative to the celibacy of the clergy, let us see what reasons are alleged for the statements so confidently put forward by many Protestant writers. The first proof adduced is based upon a passage in

* Church Hist. vol. i. p. 60.

St. Patrick's " Confession," wherein the saint states that he was " son of Calpurnius, a deacon, and grandson of Potitus, a priest;" from which the inference is sought to be deduced that in those days the clergy were not forbidden to marry, and, therefore, were Protestants, according to Mr. Whiteside's logic. Is that gentleman aware that in the Greek orthodox Catholic Church candidates for holy orders are permitted to marry before ordination? Does not every Catholic hold that the question of celibacy has nothing to do with faith—is merely a point of discipline—and the pope has the power of dispensing, either collectively or singly, in such cases? So that even were it true that the clergy were married men in the time of St. Patrick, it would only follow that a change had been made in discipline, the faith remaining completely unaltered.*

But, on the other hand, in the face of all the clear evidence which we have adduced, something better than this passage of the confession must be advanced. No writer pretends that St. Patrick was ever married; and as to his being the son of a deacon, that is not

---

* As a significant illustration of the importance of celibacy, in order to enable a clergyman to discharge his duties to the sick, may be mentioned the fact that the late Dr. Whately, in the cholera of 1832, exempted his clergymen from attendance on the dying, lest they might convey infection to their families.

an argument of much force. There is a lady resid-
ing at present, with her family, in the county Kildare; she is the daughter of a priest, who had been
an officer, left the army, and took holy orders after
his wife's death. Are we to infer therefrom that
priests in the diocese of Dublin were allowed to
marry some thirty or fifty years since?

St. Patrick's training for the ministry, shows
clearly to what religion he belonged. Mr. King tells
us,[*] that "he betook himself to the celebrated Germanus, bishop of Auxerre, in France, placing himself
under his care and direction . . . We are also told that
he spent some time with the famous St. Martin,
bishop of Tours; and having been by these prelates,
admitted to the holy orders of deacon and priest, he
travelled (by the advice it appears of St. Germanus)
to the south of France, and taking up his abode in
the island of Lerins in the Tuscan sea, remained there
for some time with the monks of a celebrated colle-
giate institution of that place, prosecuting his studies,
and growing, as we may well suppose, in piety and
Christian experience." Thus it appears, that his
patrons were two canonized saints of the Church of
Rome, whilst his teachers and companions, from

---

[*] Church Hist. vol. i. p. 27-8.

whom he learned " piety and Christian experience,"
were the monks of Lerins.

The next proof advanced by our opponents is
drawn from a canon, said to have been adopted at a
synod held by St. Patrick, in which it is enjoined
that " the clerk's wife shall not walk out without
having her head veiled." That this clause should
supply any authority against the celibacy of the
clergy, it must be shown conclusively that the word
" clerk " meant priest, and not those in minor orders.
It is upon this assumption Lord Coke proceeded
when he laid down the opinion upon which Mr.
Whiteside has dwelt with emphasis, in his late
lecture on the Irish Parliament. On looking into
the canon in which the words relative to the " clerk's
wife " occur, we find it commences with a regulation
as to the dress to be worn by clerics—" If any cleric,
from the doorkeeper up to the priest, shall be seen
without his tunic—not concealing the nakedness of
his person—and if his hair be not shorn according to
the Roman manner, and if his wife walk forth with
unveiled head, let them be despised by the laity, and
cut off from the Church."*

* The clause enjoining the Roman tonsure proves conclusively
that the canon could not have been passed before the close of the
seventh century, as the Southern Irish, up to that period, retained

Now, it is manifest that the word cleric in this canon did not include the priests, but those in the minor orders; for most assuredly we cannot imagine that priests, in the ages of Ireland's greatest sanctity, required to be restrained, by a penalty of excommunication, from wearing the dress of military men of that time—namely, a closely-fitting pantaloons, with a short cloak reaching only to the elbows, thus leaving the entire lower part of the person indecently dressed, after the fashion of an acrobat or a rope-dancer; whereas men in minor orders, not being forbidden to marry, might readily think themselves at liberty to conform in their dress to that of worldlings. Hence, we are to apply the same restriction as to the word cleric or clerk, where the passage occurs relative to "the clerk's wife," in the very same canon—that is, the wife of any person in minor orders, who, at this day is allowed to marry.

Dr. Reeves, whom we have so often quoted, sets the controversy about the meaning of "the clerk's wife" at rest for ever, by his enlightened testimony in our favour. He shows that the clause refers to

---

this peculiar tonsure. Lanigan attributes the canon to the eighth century (Eccl. Hist. vol. iv. p. 361). In any case, as a rule adopted in the early Irish Church, the force of the objection raised by Protestant writers is the same.

clerics not in holy orders, and quotes, as illustrating the passage, what Pope Gregory, in 601, prescribed for St. Augustine: "Si qui vero sunt clerici extra sacros ordines constituti, qui se continere non possunt, sortiri uxores debent, et stipendia sua, exterius accipere."[*] In the same place Dr. Reeves remarks upon "hereditary abbacies," that "we get from the Book of Armagh, a most valuable insight into the ancient economy of the Irish monasteries, in its account of the endowment of Trim. In that church there was an ecclesiastica progenies and a plebilis progenies—a religious and secular succession; the former of office, in spirituals—the latter of blood, in temporals; and both descended from the original grantor.

"The lineal transmission of the abbatial office, which appears in the Irish annals towards the close of the eighth century, probably had its origin in the usurpation, by the plebilis progenies connected with the various monasteries, of the functions of the ecclesiastica progenies, which would be the necessary result of the former omitting to keep up the succession of the latter. In such case, the tenant in possession might maintain a semblance of the clerical cha-

---

[*] "If any clerics, *who are not in holy orders*, cannot restrain their passions, let them marry," &c.—Vita Columbæ, p. 336; see Haverty's Hist. of Ireland, p. 112.

racter, by taking the tonsure and a low degree of orders."*

Many Protestant writers sedulously argued that hereditary abbacies were an irresistible proof that the clergy were married men: this last extract supplies them with new food for thought, and directs the current of their imagination into channels where historic facts abound, and will serve, we trust, to purify the unwholesome and turbid waters of prejudice and ignorance.

We have already shown that the great and illustrious saints of Ireland, St. Columkille and St. Columbanus, advocated strenuously the celibacy of the clergy. It is an old maxim: "the way to virtue by precept is long, by example is short."

As a practical illustration of this clerical virtue, we shall cite an account of the closing scenes of the life of St. Columbkille. The Rev. R. King† beautifully describes the dying hour of this saint, and gives the following extract from Adamnan;—

" This, then," continues Adamnan, " was the close of our illustrious patron's life; this, his entrance on his recompense; who now, according to the sentence of the Scripture, admitted as a companion to former

* Vita Columbæ, Notes, p. 335.
† Church Hist. vol. i. p. 93-4.

saints in their triumphs, joined with apostles and prophets, numbered with the company of the thousands, arrayed in white, of the saints who have washed their robes in the Lamb's blood, follows the Lamb for his leader, a spotless virgin free from every stain, through the grace of our Lord Jesus Christ himself, who, with the Father, hath all honor, power, praise, and glory and dominion for ever, in the unity of the Holy Ghost, world without end. Amen." Such was Columba's end—such the recital of it given by his distinguished successor Adamnan." Mr. King, then, in a marginal note in reference to Adamnan's Life of St. Columbkille, endeavours to obscure the facts which he could not suppress. " The narrative," he tells us, " is not Romish in its character." A little further on, he says of St. Columbkille, in addition to his being " a spotless virgin, free from every stain," that " he exhibited in his life the greatest mortification and self-denial, sometimes fasting for whole days and watching for whole nights; and thus even in the winter season, while others were enjoying, after the labours of the day, the comforts of repose and slumber, he would betake himself to the church, for the purpose of having secret communion with God in the still and lonely hours of darkness.. He applied himself, as his biographer, Cummian, remarks, to fastings, and watchings, and prayers, meditations, also, upon the Scriptures, preaching of the faith, and other labours of love, with an incredible untiring earnestness of mind." We read, also, that "his bed consisted of nothing more than a hide stretched out upon the bare ground, and he had, like the patriarch Jacob, a stone for a pillow."

It is amusing to find Mr. King, whilst thus delineating the character of St. Columbkille, yet undertaking to tell us that "the narrative has nothing Romish" about it. We are not aware that the Protestant saints have ever been remarkable as "spotless virgins, who devote their lives to fastings, the greatest mortifications and self-denials." We rather fancy that these are the virtues prized in the Catholic Church now, as in the days of Columbkille.

Venerable Bede (who lived in the eighth century), bears similar testimony to the virtuous lives of the successors of Columbkille; for he says: " Whatever kind of person he himself was, this we know of him for certain, that he left successors distinguished for their great chastity, divine love, and strict attention to their rules of discipline."[*]

* King's Church Hist. vol. i. p. 105.

Section II.

RESPECT FOR THE SACRED SCRIPTURES.

Protestant writers adduce, as a triumphant proof that the early Irish saints were members of their Church, the fact that they entertained the greatest reverence for the Sacred Scriptures—that they studied the Bible assiduously, and that their writings,—as, for instance, those of St. Columbkille and St. Columbanus,—are full of quotations from the word of God; hence they infer they could not have been Catholics. " It is believed," says Mr. O'Hagan, in his noble defence of Father Petcherine, " by multitudes in these countries that the Catholic Church is the enemy of the Holy Bible,—that she fears and hates its divine teachings, and would utterly destroy it if she could. This belief has been sedulously circulated, sometimes through ignorance, sometimes through fraud, and sometimes through fanaticism; fostered by the teachings of an anti-Catholic literature, enforced from the Protestant pulpit and by the Protestant press, and entertained with unquestioning assurance by crowds of the simple Protestant people.

The Catholic Church is not the enemy of the Bible. I affirm it, and I shall prove it. . . . . . She has been the guardian of its purity and the preserver of its existence through the chances and changes of eighteen hundred years. In the gloom of the Catacombs, and the splendour of the Basilica, she cherished that Holy Book with equal reverence. When she saw the seed of Christianity sown in the blood of the martyrs, and braved the persecutions of the despots of the world—and when those despots bowed before the symbol of Redemption, and she was lifted from her earthly humbleness, and 'reared her mitred head' in courts and palaces, it was equally the object of her unceasing care. She gathered together its scattered fragments, separated the true word of inspiration from the spurious inventions of presumptuous and deceitful men; made its teachings and its history familiar to her children in her noble liturgy; translated it into the language which was familiar to every one who could read at all; asserted its divine authority in her councils; maintained its canonical integrity against all gainsayers, and transmitted it from age to age, as the precious inheritance of the Christian people. The saints whom she most reveres were its sagest commentators; and of the army of her white-robed martyrs whom she still commemorates on her festal days, there are many who reached their immortal crowns by refusing, on the rack and in the flames, to desecrate or deny the Holy Book of God."

In these eloquent and truthful words, Mr. O'Hagan refuted the charges of opposition to the word of God on the part of the Catholic Church. It is true that at all times, the Church has claimed the right to restrict or extend the perusal of the sacred volume, and will not suffer that precious deposit to be misconstrued or explained away, by thrusting it into the hands of the ignorant and ungodly, and saying to them—Interpret it for yourselves, bring your own private spirit to bear upon its meaning, and adjust its teachings to your own views, prejudices or principles. We confidently appeal to the results of these opposite modes of dealing with the Scripture, to prove which course is most conducive to the preservation of the authority, reverence, and veneration with which the word of God should be treated by all believers.* What do we find to be the case in

---

* Our desire has been to treat the questions discussed in these pages, in a historical rather than a' controversial manner; yet it may not be amiss, in referring to the different teachings of the Catholic and Protestant Church, relative to the indiscriminate reading and interpretation of the Sacred Scriptures, to notice briefly the views advocated by those who differ from us. The doctrine

England at the present day?—that the English
people are called upon to reject the authority of the
Old Testament altogether, at the bidding of Dr.
Colenso, and that his arguments will also prove
fatal with those who adopt them, to the claims of the
New Testament, as an inspired book. The bishop
of Natal writes, in his work on the Pentateuch:† " for
myself, if I cannot find the means of doing away
with my present difficulties, I see not how I can
retain my episcopal office, in the discharge of which, I
must require from others a solemn declaration that
' they unfeignedly believe all the canonical Scriptures
of the Old and New Testament,' which, with the
evidence now before me, it is impossible wholly to

of the Protestant Church is—that God has given His revealed
word into our hands, with the right and the obligation, upon the
part of each individual, to study it, and thereby to form his code of
belief. One argument appears to us to dispose very readily of this
position. If Christ left to the members of his Church the command to form their creed upon their private interpretation of the
Sacred Scriptures, and if such were the means of salvation which
He selected for the Church, then two things plainly follow—first,
that He left His Church for fourteen hundred years without those
necessary means, and thereby falsified His own words: "Going,
therefore, teach all nations, and behold I am with you all days,
even to the consummation of the world."—(St. Matt. xxviii. 28.)
Secondly, that Christ, commanded impossible things to His disciples, as until after the invention of printing, in the middle of the
fifteenth century, it was clearly impossible for the members of the
Church to procure copies of the Bible for their individual study.

† Preface, page xii.

L

believe in." Again, he says, "This conviction which I have arrived at, of the *certainty* of the ground on which the *main* argument of my book rests, (viz., the proof that the account of the Exodus, whatever value it may have, *is not historically true,**) must be my excuse to the reader, for the manner in which I have conducted the inquiry."

These open words of infidelity, by a bishop of the Established Church, express also the feelings of many of the educated classes, as Dr. Colenso assures us.

"There can be no doubt,† that a very wide-spread distrust does exist, among the intelligent society in England, as to the soundness of the ordinary view of Scripture inspiration. It is rather secretly felt, than openly expressed; though it is sufficiently exhibited to the eye of a reflecting man, in many outward signs of the times, and in none more painfully than in the fact, which has been lamented by more than one of the English bench of bishops, and which every colonial bishop must still more sorrowfully confess, that the great body of the more intelligent students of our univerities, no longer come forward to devote themselves to the service of the Church, but

---

* Preface, p. xviii. The italics are Dr. Colenso's.
† Preface, p. xxiii.

are drafted off into other professions." Thus we see, as
the result of this indiscriminate reading and interpret-
ing of God's holy word, that many of the intelligent
classes in England reject the authority of the Scriptures, and will not enter the ministry because, in the
words of Dr. Colenso, 'tis impossible wholly to believe
in the word of truth itself, the inspired Scriptures.[*]
As for Dr. Colenso's scruple about retaining his episcopal office, he seems to have got over that, as the
following lines from *Punch* will show; they are quite
in the spirit of Horace—" Quid vetat ridentem dicere
verum ?"

THE NATAL CORRESPONDENCE.

MY DEAR COLENSO,
                                With regret,
We, hierarchs, in conclave met,
Beg you, you most disturbing writer,
To take off your colonial mitre.
This course we press upon you strongly.
Believe me, yours most truly,
                                        LONGLEY.
    Lambeth.

---

[*] The Rev. Dr. Manning, in his Sermons on Ecclesiastical Sub-
jects, p. 25, says: "The more I have studied the religious and
political history of England since the Anglican Reformation, and
the more I have observed the currents of thought—the dominant
tendencies in English society at this day—the more I have become
convinced that the English people are upon an inclined plane. Men
may strive to retard their descent, but it is inevitable. The laws of
Nature are not more irresistible and unerring than the law which
generates unbelief from the first principle of private judgment.
Even in our own lifetime, the advance of indifference, rationalism,
infidelity, secularism, and atheism, both objective and subjective,
is vast and perceptible."

II.

My dear Archbishop,

> To resign
> That Zulu diocese of mine,
> And own myself a heathen dark,
> Because I've doubts about Noah's ark,
> And feel it right to tell all men so,
> Is not the course for

> > Yours,

> > > Colenso.

Kensington.

As a contrast to the impiety and infidelity of which Dr. Colenso is the spokesman, let us turn to the manner in which the Holy Bible is loved and venerated in the Church to which we belong. Would any member of the Catholic Church be tolerated for one moment, were he to deny the slightest title in the entire Bible? Not one; he would be excommunicated by the very fact of such a denial. Would any priest or any bishop be countenanced in our Church, who should proclaim that "it was impossible wholly to believe in the sacred Scriptures?" Not for an hour. Therefore, when Columbkille and Columbanus, illustrious missioners and anointed teachers of the people, insisted upon the authority of the word of God, as above all question or doubt, they acted as the Catholic Church has ever done, in protecting from irreverent questioning or cavil, the sacred deposit of the faith, left to the Church, to be guarded as a precious treasure, and not profaned, to be reverenced as the inspired record of God's dealings with man—a record which being God's own work, must, like himself, be true, without the shadow of ignorance or error. It is reserved for modern times,"and a modern religion, to advocate the liberty of falsifying the word of God, and to allow each person to admit or deny whatever portion may suit his fancy, or clash with his prejudices. That the Irish ecclesiastics in expounding the sacred Scriptures were careful to have their studies guided by the teachings of the Catholic Church, and not by their own individual opinions, is evinced by a fact mentioned in King's History.* "The legends of Kiaran of Saigir . . . . relate that this saint, when thirty years old, went to Rome, and spent there twenty years reading the divine Scriptures, and collecting copies of them." Thus did the venerable Kiaran seek in Rome, the centre of orthodoxy, the authoritative exposition of the inspired word, and little dreamt of being at liberty to interpret as he pleased, the solemn messages of revelation from God to man.

We have now discussed all the points with which we proposed to deal. We have passed in review the

* Church Hist. vol. i. p. 323.

teachings of the ancient Christian Church in Ireland on the blessed Eucharist, the sacrifice of the Mass, Confession, Purgatory, prayers for the dead, the invocation of the saints, the veneration for the Mother of God, the constant use of the sign of the cross, miracles, the doctrine on fasting, on the supremacy of the pope, the celibacy of the clergy, and the respect due to the sacred Scriptures.

This brings our humble labours to a close. We have laid fairly and candidly before the reader our authorities throughout the investigation. Regretting very much, as we most sincerely do, that so important an inquiry should not have been conducted by those whose abilities and leisure would enable them to enlighten every obscurity, and clothe every dry incident in the luxuriance of polished style, we, in lieu of anything better, have simply made an effort in the right direction. Should this publication be successful in calling forth essays more worthy of our interesting theme, Irish Catholics, proud of their country and their ancient creed, may be supplied with eloquent and truthful histories of the ages of faith.

APPENDIX.

THE FESTOLOGY OF ÆNGUS.

We have already* briefly alluded to this Festology. If the Danes in their many ravages had succeeded in destroying every record of the ancient Irish Church, save only this one, it would be quite sufficient to make us fully acquainted with the teachings of the Church of Erinn, in the days of her greatest glory. Hence, we deem it advisable to give here a description of that important manuscript. We take the outline from a lengthened account, contained in O'Curry's MS. Materials of Irish History.† Those who can lay their hands upon O'Curry's work, would be amply repaid by an attentive perusal of the pages which are here summarized.

The Festology is contained in the celebrated Leabhar Breac, which was compiled about the year 1400. The author's name was Ængus, who resided for a considerable time near the town of Monasterevan, in the Queen's county. Ængus composed his Felire, or Festology, in the reign of Aedh Oirdnidhe, who was monarch of Erinn from the year 793 to the year 817. Ængus commenced his poem in

* See pages 14 and 67.
† MS. Materials, p. 363, etc.

Offaly, the present Queen's county, and finished it at
Tallacht, in the county Dublin. The cause and object of
writing this Festology are stated thus: One time that
Ængus went to the church of Cuil Bennchair, he saw, he
says, a grave there, and angels from heaven, constantly
descending and ascending to and from it. Ængus asked
the priest of the church who the person was that was
buried in this grave; the priest answered, that it was a
poor old man who formerly lived at the place. What good
did he do? said Ængus. I saw no particular good by
him, said the priest, but that his customary practice was to
recount and invoke the saints of the world, as far as he
could remember them, at his going to bed and getting up, in
accordance with the custom of the old devotees. Ah! my
God, said Ængus, he who would make a poetical composition
in praise of the saints, should doubtless have a high reward,
when so much has been vouchsafed to this old devotee. And
Ængus then commenced his poem on the spot. The composition consists properly of three parts. The first, after invoking
our Saviour, " Sanctify, O Christ! my words," &c., goes on,
in beautiful and forcible language, to give a glowing account
of the tortures and sufferings of the early Christian martyrs;
how the names of the persecutors are forgotten, whilst the
names of their victims are remembered with honour, veneration, and affection; how Pilate's wife is forgotten, and the
Blessed Virgin Mary is remembered and honoured, from the
uttermost bounds of the earth to its centre. Even in our

own country the enduring supremacy of the Church of Christ is made manifest; for Tara, says the poet, had become abandoned under the vain glory of its kings, while Armagh remains the populous seat of dignity, piety, and learning; Cruachain, the royal residence of the kings of Connacht, is deserted, while Clonmacnoise resounds with the dashing of chariots and the tramp of multitudes, to honour the shrine of St. Ciaran; the royal palace of Aillinn, in Leinster, has passed away, while the church of St. Brigid, at Kildare, remains in dazzling splendour; Emania, the royal palace of Ulster, has disappeared, while the holy Kevin's church at Glendalough, remains in full glory; the monarch Laeghaire's pride was extinguished, while St. Patrick's name continued to shine with growing lustre.

In the third division of his work, Ængus explains its arrangement, and directs the faithful how to read and use it; and he says, that though great the number be, he has only been able to enumerate the princes of the saints in it. He recommends it to the pious study of the faithful, and points out the spiritual benefits to be gained by reading or reciting it. He says, that he has travelled far and near to collect the names of the saints; that for those of foreign nations, he has consulted St. Ambrose, St. Jerome, and Eusebius; and that from "the countless hosts of the illuminated books of Erinn," he has collected the festivals of the Irish saints. He then says, that having already mentioned and invoked the saints at their respective festival days, he will now invoke them in classes or bands,

M

under certain heads or leaders; and this he does in the following order: the ancients under Noah, the prophets under Isaiah, the patriarchs under Abraham, the apostles and disciples under Peter, the wise, or learned men, under Paul, the martyrs under Stephen, the spiritual directors under old Paul, the virgins of the world under the Blessed Virgin Mary, the holy bishops of Rome under Peter, the noble saints of Erinn under St. Patrick, the saints of Scotland under St. Columbkille; and the last great division of the saintly virgins of Erinn, under the holy St. Brigid of Kildare. The sacred bard continues then in an eloquent strain, to beseech the mercy of the Saviour for himself and all mankind, through the merits and sufferings of the saints whom he has enumerated, through the merits of their dismembered bodies—their bodies pierced with lances, their wounds, their groans, their relics, their blanched countenances, their bitter tears; through all the sacrifices offered of the Saviour's own Body and Blood, as it is in heaven, upon the holy altars; through the Blood that flowed from the Saviour's own side, through his Humanity and through his Divinity, in unity with the Holy Spirit and the Heavenly Father.

Again, he beseeches Jesus, through the intercession of his Mother, to save him, as Jacob was saved from the hands of his brother. He beseeches Jesus again, through the intercession of the heavenly household, to be saved, as he saved St. Patrick from the poisoned drink at Tara, and St. Kevin of Glendaloch, from the perils of the mountains.

O'Curry concludes his lengthened description of this very remarkable work, in these interesting words: "I have trespassed on your patience at such unreasonable length with the details of this extraordinary poem, merely for the purpose of showing you, that the gifted writer could not be set down as a mere ignorant or superstitious monk, but that he was a man deeply read in the Holy Scriptures, and in the civil and ecclesiastical history of the world, and more particularly that part of it which was contained in what he so enthusiastically calls ' the host of the books of Erinn.'

"It is no part of the purpose of these lectures to enter into doctrinal discussions on the merits of our ancient sacred writings; but taking this Festology of St. Ængus as a purely historic tract, largely interwoven with the early history of Erinn, I almost think no other country in Europe possesses a national document of so important a character."

O'Curry mentions with justifiable pride and satisfaction, that he was the first person in modern times that discovered the value of the contents of this work of the eighth century, which so plainly sets forth the faith of our fathers."

> "Faith of our Fathers! days of old
>   Within our hearts speak gallantly;
> For ages thou hast stood by us,
>   Dear Faith! and now we'll stand by thee.
> Faith of our fathers! Holy Faith!
> We will be true to thee till death."

THE END.